Finding Your Way

AMY K. McCLUNG

For information, contact the publisher, Hot Tree Publishing.

WWW.HOTTREEPUBLISHING.COM

EDITING: HOT TREE EDITING

COVER DESIGNER: CLAIRE SMITH

FORMATTING: RMGraphX

ISBN: 978-1-925853-54-4

List Of Books

SOUTHERN DEVOTION SERIES
For the Love of Gracie
Curves in the Road
Complicated Relationships
Twisted Fate

STAND-ALONES
A Little Spark
Across the Way
Still You
Finding Your Way

*This book is dedicated to anyone who has ever felt
the crippling fear of anxiety. Know that you're not alone,
you're not crazy, you are strong, and no matter how scary
it may seem, you will get through it.*

Chapter One

As I glanced out over the vast span of water in front of me, I imagined sitting on the shore with my arm wrapped around the beauty beside me. Her pixie-cut hairstyle matched her Tinkerbell laugh. As the sun began to set, she peered up at me through long dark lashes. Leaning down, I gently kissed her, tasting the bubble gum lip gloss she applied earlier. "I love you," she whispered against my lips. Sighing, I pressed my forehead against hers. "I love you."

The dream was the same every night. And every morning I woke up missing Connie even more. Two years ago, almost to the day, she died from a congenital heart defect. I'd met her by chance through my best friend Brady who, at the same time, was dating her best friend Marie. Our romance was short lived, but in the small amount of time we had, I fell hard. As Connie would have wanted, I did my best to live life to the fullest, but some days were harder than others. Her image haunted me everywhere. Each time I saw her beautiful face, I ached to touch her again.

Ludington, Michigan, was my home, and I never had a chance to show Connie. Marie was on the road trip of a lifetime, traveling the United States and Canada. She passed through Michigan just before heading to Canada to meet Connie, the cousin of her lifelong best friend Jayce. Marie met Brady in Ludington before she met Connie, so the timeline never matched up for us. I had planned to propose to her on that very beach, the shores of Lake Michigan. Though it wasn't a place we shared, it was the spot where I met Marie, which brought me to Connie. For months I'd saved to buy the perfect ring, walking by the jewelry store twice a week to make sure it was there. Finally, the store owner waved me in and asked me if I wanted to purchase it. "Still saving up, but if it's still here when I have the money, I'll know it's fate."

With a sad smile, probably of pity, she reached into the case and brought the ring out. "Let's not leave true love up to fate. Fate can be a cruel bitch sometimes." These words spilled forth from a sweet lady who had to be at least eighty. If I hadn't heard them for myself, I never would have believed she uttered such vulgarity. "I'm going to put this in the safe, and when you have the money, you come back and get it.

I never stepped foot in that store again. Being a heartbroken man, I couldn't face her. Brady went in my stead and took cash I'd wanted her to have since I cost her a sale. Living in a small town, she'd heard the news and refused the money, asking me to come back one day when

I was ready.

For thirty years I'd been a player, jumping from one girl to the next. Never once did love factor in until that pixie-haired girl walked into my life.

* * *

"Brady?" I called out as I knocked on his open door. A chorus of moans and grunts welcomed me. "Shit." I turned to leave just as Brady stepped out of his room. "You're dressed." Genuinely surprised yet thankful at not receiving the full monty.

"Yeah, man, we're moving furniture in here."

"Is that what the kids are calling it these days?" I smirked. *Damn I missed sex.* For a year after losing Connie I stayed abstinent, and when I finally got wasted enough to not think about her, it was bad. Bad like prom night sex between two Amish virgins. Not that Amish people are bad at sex I'm sure, but I imagine they don't see a lot of porn to know where things go. Well… never mind, bad subject.

"It's true. The bed was by the window directly facing the sun in the morning, making it suck to try and sleep in on the weekends." Dawn poked her head out and grinned.

"Hey, Manny Banany."

Groan. "You're never going to stop calling me that are you?"

Pinching my cheeks, she smushed her lips up. "Not since I know you hate it so much."

Brady and Dawn had been together for eight months, and it was healthy for him. His relationship with Marie had been doomed from the start, but he gave it his all, trying to make it work. The final nail in their relationship coffin was Jayce, Marie's lifelong best friend. After Marie met Brady, Jayce decided it was a good time to let her know he had deeper feelings for her. Brady found it hard to compete with a best friend who knew his girl better than anyone else could ever hope to. I met Marie the same day Brady did. We truly bonded after Connie's death, when I finished the road trip with Marie. At first it was difficult to maintain friendships with both, when Brady was so miserable without her and Marie was blissfully happy with Jayce. Dawn's arrival in Brady's life made things easier on all of us.

Dawn had become a good friend to me, even if she did give me the worst nickname ever. When she first met Brady, she was an elementary school teacher. Shortly after they met, she was laid off due to budget cuts. The salon in town was up for sale at the time, one she frequented and knew was successful, so she used her savings to purchase it. The switch in careers was drastic. She had to go back to school to get her cosmetology license, but she was a people person and wanted to be her own boss for a change. As we got to know each other, every so often she would try to hook me up with one of her clients. And each time I turned her down because there's nothing more frustrating than a blind date that goes bad.

"We're going down to the beach for a swim this afternoon. Want to join us?" Dawn asked with a gleam in her eye. I knew that look, she had a setup in mind.

"Stop trying to hook me up, Dawn. I can find my own women."

Brady chuckled. "Back in the day maybe, but you've lost your flare a little there."

"What I lost was my wingman. All for the love of a good woman." Cringing, we both looked at Dawn to see if she caught what I meant, but she smiled along, probably assuming we were referring to her.

"My friend Perry is going to be there. She's sweet."

"Manny and Perry? People will think we're a salon pun. That combo will never work."

Exasperated, Dawn flung her hands in the air. "I give up. It's a shame because hotness like yours shouldn't go to waste."

Music went off in my pocket, saving me from the conversation. Still rolling my eyes over the Manny Perry idea, I stepped outside to answer my phone. "Hola, chica!"

"Hello, my friend. Long time no talk." Marie and I hadn't spoken on the phone in six months. Emails, texted pictures, and the occasional tagged Facebook post or tweet was the extent of our communication. She was a relatively new mom, and it was hard to keep in touch these days.

"How is my beautiful goddaughter?"

"Perfect as always; I wanted to call you about the anniversary this week. Connie's parents have asked us to come up to see them. Jayce and I were hoping you'd go with us."

"You want me to meet you in Canada?"

"Well, we were thinking we'd drive and swing by to get you instead. We determined it would be easier to carry all the baby stuff by car rather than plane. Plus, you and I'd get a taste of old times." Her voice softened to a whisper. "I know it isn't the best idea to show up in Brady's town with my family. But Jayce wants to do a road trip, and I couldn't say no."

Hesitation settled in my soul as I considered the ramifications of Marie and Brady seeing one another again. After our last visit, it caused a rift between him and Dawn. They'd been together for two months when we went to visit Marie in the hospital after she had Constance. Brady didn't tell Dawn he went, and two months later it came up in conversation accidentally. Dawn accused him of hiding it from her because he was still in love with Marie. It turned into a huge debacle with me smack in the middle of the fight. I thought for sure they'd never come back from it. In the end, it was for the best because it made him realize his feelings for her, and they decided to move in together.

Just in time to make things awkward, Brady opened the door and said, "Yo, Manny Banany, are you coming or going?"

Marie snorted. "Manny Banany? When did Brady start calling you that?"

"A few moments before I killed him. It's his girlfriend's nickname for me. I'm at their house." I pointed at my phone and then held up one finger to ask him to give me a minute.

Quiet filled the line for a moment. "They live together now? It must be serious." Her tone implied a hint of jealousy.

"Not as serious as married with a baby but close enough." I believed Marie cared deeply for Brady, and she had a difficult time making her choice, but she made it. When she let Brady go and chose Jayce, she no longer had any right to be jealous of anyone he dated.

"Touché."

"I've got a little time off work coming up, so let me check my workload and get back to you. It would be good to see you and Jayce again. Call you tomorrow?"

"Sounds great. Bye, Manny Banany."

"I seriously hate all of you." Laughter erupted through the speaker. I hung up the phone and released my annoyance by rolling my eyes.

* * *

The idea of Marie and Jayce being in town where Dawn resided wasn't Brady's favorite idea. With a talent for making things worse, after I told Marie I'd go, she asked if we could all have dinner together. If looks could kill, I'd have been struck dead instantly when I voiced the suggestion to Brady. After a little time to think he admitted it would be nice to see them again. Plus, he promised they'd be friends, and he wanted to honor his word.

On the day of arrival, Marie kept me updated on their distance away, so when she was within thirty minutes, I could leave to meet her at the hotel right outside the city limits. My loft wasn't big enough for three adults and a baby, but I did offer it as a gesture. If she had taken me up on it, I would've slept on the couch and given them my bed.

When they were three hours away, I called Brady to warn him of their pending arrival. He'd been giving me the "I'm fine" speech every time I mentioned it, but I knew this would be weird. Dawn wasn't exactly thrilled about seeing them either, but she was putting on a brave face. For Dawn's part, I assumed she agreed to it so she could meet the woman who brought out such jealousy in her.

Two hours before their arrival, I drove over to the local superstore and picked up a few little gifts for my goddaughter since I hadn't had a chance to spoil her properly. Facebook was my connection to the little girl as I watched her grow up in pictures. One hundred fifty dollars later, I felt sufficient spoiling had been done.

Exiting the store, I got the "We're an hour away" text from Marie. Since I wasn't far from the hotel they'd be staying at, I decided to park and grab a snack at the fast-food restaurant next door while I waited.

Along with the bite to eat, I passed the time going through my social media accounts and catching up on the latest news. As time dragged on, I began to play mindless games on my phone instead. On my… well I'd lost count of the rounds of solitaire I'd played, I glanced up to check the time just as Marie's SUV pulled into the hotel. I grinned as I spotted her through the window.

Tossing away my trash, I sprinted through the parking lot, across the entryway to the hotel, and pounced on her the moment she stepped out of the car. A gasp and then laughter greeted me. "Manny!" she exclaimed, embracing me as tightly as possible. I felt her body shake with sobs, a reaction very normal for her.

"Why are you crying, loco?" I smoothed her hair back with my fingers and wiped away the tears with my thumbs.

"I've missed you so much. And now seeing you, I miss Connie even more too. She should be here, in your arms." Even though several months had gone by since we'd seen each other in person, it felt like only yesterday we were mourning Connie the same way. When Marie was around, the pain felt so fresh, but it was also easier to handle, if that made any sense.

"Don't make me cry, chica." Pulling her back into my arms, I waved as Jayce stepped out of the car and tended to baby Constance.

"She's hormonal, Manny. Forgive her." I watched him work to unbuckle their baby daughter and then turned back to Marie.

"Hormonal?" My eyes widened as the truth set in. "Are you pregnant again?"

Marie's face scrunched up in what could be described as a look of sheer pain, she nodded. "A month."

"Congratulations! Damn, you two don't waste time."

Jayce shrugged and then lifted the car seat up before shutting the car door. "It was a pleasant surprise. One Marie is still adjusting to I think." *She's not the only one.*

"Do you two want to get some rest? I can take Constance for a bit." For a small woman, Marie gave a powerful hug. When she flung herself at me, I barely kept my stance. "I assume that's a yes?"

"You have no idea how much help it would be. Thank you!" Kissing my cheek, she squeezed me once more.

Leaving Marie and Jayce at the hotel, I loaded Constance, car seat and all, into the back seat of my car. Ten miles away, just off the shoreline of Lake Michigan, my apartment was not company ready. Luckily the current company wasn't picky, so I could watch her and clean at the same time.

We settled on three hours before they would return, so you can imagine my surprise when someone knocked on my door thirty minutes later. I thought it must be regretful parents. "She's fine!" I exclaimed as I opened the door.

"Who's fine?" Brady asked, looking around.

Well, this won't be awkward at all. "Constance."

Concern marked Brady's features since the Constance I normally referenced was the love who died. "Manny, have you been drinking?"

"*Baby* Constance. Marie and Jayce arrived in town, and I took her for a bit to give them time to rest from the long drive. Would you like to come in and see her?"

"Why not? I mean, it's not weird at all that she's the baby of my ex-girlfriend and the man who stole her right from under me." Meeting my eyes, he smirked and added, "Not that I hold a grudge."

"Right. Well, she's here. Come on in while she's being good."

Constance beamed when she spotted Brady smiling above her. She lifted her pudgy arms and said, "Da." *Shit.* A simple word, a nonword really, sent Brady into shock. It only lasted a minute before he had her in his arms.

"Hi, sweet girl. I'm your… Uncle Brady?" We exchanged a look and shrugs, figuring what could it hurt. Googly eyes, baby talk, smushy-face noises, the two of us were pudding in this chick's hands. Well, I suppose she was in our hands, but either way we were whipped.

"Can you watch her while I clean?" Sure, I could do it myself, but with someone else's help, I could get it done even quicker.

"How long are they going to be in town?" Brady took a dig at my bachelor pad cleanliness. After giving him the one-finger salute, he waved the white flag of surrender, a dirty diaper in this case. "Start with disposing of this. I'll watch Constance."

As I ran around the house, I heard Brady talking to Constance, telling her about his day and about how he knew her mom. She couldn't understand what he was saying, but I knew it made him feel good to talk about it. One day he'd be a great dad. I knew part of him looked at Constance and wondered how his life would've been different if she'd been his instead. She wasn't conceived while they were dating, there was no paternity question when Marie found out she was pregnant, but I knew he considered the what-ifs of her choosing him instead.

Constance's tinkling laugh caught my attention. I peered around the corner to check on them and saw Brady giving her raspberries on her stomach. Her tiny legs were kicking as she roared with laughter. Brady looked so natural playing with her.

Two hours later my house was company friendly just

in time for a knock on the door. Stepping into the house, Marie's gaze landed on Brady playing with her child, and it was easy to see the love for Brady still resonated within her. Pushing past her to scoop his daughter up, it seemed Jayce noticed too.

"Good to see you, Marie." A small smile teased at Brady's lips. He barely tried to hide his enjoyment at the look of annoyance on Jayce's face. His reaction might be immature, but it wasn't exactly unwarranted considering their past.

"You too. How's Dawn?" Asking about the girlfriend was a nice deflector in my opinion, though Jayce rolled his eyes.

"Great. Manny said he wanted to take you guys to the beach. Maybe we could all go. Take a walk out to the lighthouse?"

Checking his watch, Jayce replied, "How's now? Call her up to meet us."

Brady stepped away to call Dawn. "He's great with Constance, had her laughing like crazy."

Jayce kissed his daughter's head. "She loves to laugh."

"She loves her Uncle Manny too," Marie added.

Brady came back in the room. "Dawn will have to meet us later. She has a few more clients this afternoon."

"Da," Constance called out to Brady.

Jayce's jaw tensed as he stared down my best friend. Sliding into the space between them, I reached for my goddaughter. "Come here, sweet girl. Uncle Manny missed you terribly."

"Da!" she called out with a giggle. Jayce relaxed this time with the realization his daughter wasn't calling her mother's ex-boyfriend daddy. She was simply using the only word she knew currently. "Da man, that's who I am." The air in the room began to thin as the tensions died down.

"Let's head to the water. I want to show Jayce Lake Michigan." Marie wrapped her arm around mine and tugged me toward the door. "I want to show him where we first met."

"We met there too," Brady reminded her.

"True. And that led me to two amazing friendships." She wrapped her free arm around Brady's bicep. A minute later she released her hold on Brady. Jayce didn't seem fazed by the contact, but for some reason she appeared hurt.

"I'll drive," I offered. Grabbing my keys, I held the door as everyone trekked outside.

And just like that, we were in the car on our way to see the beach and having an awkward as hell moment. Brady sat in the front with me while Jayce and Marie sat on either side of the car seat in the back. Marie and I talked while the other two stared out their respective windows with tight jawlines.

A concrete path, almost a mile long, led to the lighthouse. Along the way were markers with the distance you had left to go. Since Dawn had a few more hours at work, we made the trip without her and agreed to eat dinner together in a bit instead.

Being the gentleman as always, Brady offered to take pictures of the family enjoying their first outing there together.

I admired how strong he was being. If Connie hadn't died but left me for another man instead, I don't know that I would've been so accommodating.

"They're a cute family. Are you with him?" Standing next to me was a vision in white, well, a white T-shirt at least. She was a few inches shorter than me with curvy hips and long legs. Sunlight bounced off her golden locks as sparkling green eyes looked up at me. Her rosy pink lips puckered with curiosity.

One step backward and I began to lose my balance on the ramp just before the lighthouse landing. The beauty grasped my wrist to steady me. Electric sparks danced over our joined hands.

"Thanks," I said after regaining my balance with her help.

"So, he's not your boyfriend?" she asked with a smirk.

"What? Him?" I point to Brady. "No, we're just friends. I mean, he's not my type. I'm… going to shut up."

Tucking a strand of hair behind her ear, she gazed up at me beneath dark lashes. My mind flashed back to a memory of Connie doing the same thing, giving me that look, and the same feelings stirred within me.

I gazed at this woman with my mouth open, unable to speak, trying to stand on weakened knees. Soon she'd probably run for the hills or jump in the lake or put out a restraining order on me.

"Hey." Following the sound of Marie's voice, I turned to see what she needed. "Can you hold onto the stroller while we go up in the lighthouse?"

By the time I turned around, I saw the woman had gone halfway back down the walkway. Part of me wanted to dash after her, get her name and number. A small part of me felt guilty for finding her attractive. The timing seemed the most inappropriate with the anniversary of losing Connie.

Mesmerized by the sway of her hips, I couldn't take my eyes off her. Pausing, she turned, saw me gawking, and gave an adorable wave.

"Earth to Manny!" Marie waved a hand in front of my face. "Was she a friend of yours?"

"I have no idea." I didn't know her, that I was sure of. Currently though my mind couldn't focus on finding the words to answer Marie.

Sliding her hand over mine, Marie took hold of the stroller. "Well, run after her and get a number." My feet were glued in place, and it took a shove from Marie for me to get moving.

Taking her advice, I took off in a mad sprint to catch up. Dashing around people, I kept apologizing and excusing myself as I jumped in front of them. If I hadn't been careful, I would've ended up falling into the lake, and because I was lucky, I'd missed the large boulders lining the walkway.

At the parking lot, I spotted her getting into a Jeep with Florida tags. Before I could reach her, she was on her way down the street. With out-of-state tags, she was more than likely a tourist, which meant the odds of seeing her again were low.

Apparently, my flirting skills died a long time ago. At the edge of the sand was an empty bench where I took a seat to wallow in grief of my deceased mojo. Back in the day, Brady and I were wingmen for each other. The day he met Marie, everything changed. With Dawn, well, those two were lifers whether they realized it, or not.

"Did you score her number?" Brady asked. Peering down the sidewalk, I noticed Jayce and Marie were still walking the path several feet back. Lowering his voice, Brady said, "I had to ditch them. There's only so much I can take."

"No worries. She was driving off when I got down here. Brady, I haven't been so attracted to a woman in two years. I had begun to think I never would be again."

"Maybe you needed a jump start." We were interrupted by his phone ringing, so I stared off into the water while he answered. Only hearing part of the conversation, I deduced Dawn was ready to leave work and meet for dinner.

Dawn offered to grab a couple of pizzas on her way home, so we could meet up at Brady's for comfort. Introductions were made, Dawn cooed over Constance for several minutes before finally giving her back. The green-eyed monster peeked out a few times in Marie while watching Dawn and Brady with the baby. She caught me watching her, in judgment, and shrugged sheepishly when I shook my head.

Watching the two couples interact made me lonely. In the empty seat next to me, I could see Constance. Her tinkling laughter sang to me, her porcelain skin cooled me, her whispered words lulled me. Brady's voice dragged me back to reality.

"Dawn, your friend Perry is on her way over. She said she forgot your tip today."

Rolling my eyes, I said, "This better not be a setup."

"Relax, Manny Banany. She was a bit flustered when I saw her earlier. She's a regular and hates to feel like she stiffed me. No setup." And a knock on the door came just as she had her hands full. "Can you get that?"

There better not be some overly made up, scantily clad woman behind this door. *Damn. Never thought I'd wish for that.* Sighing, I opened the door to find my dream girl standing on the porch.

"Oh. Hello again. I'm…"

"Don't say Perry," I begged.

Scrunching her face up, her cringe matched mine. "My full name is Peregrin. My parents were LOTR fans."

"*Lord of the Rings*? Are you shitting me?"

"Rarely do I shit people. In fact, I've never shit anyone." And even talking shit with each other was sort of a turn on with this girl.

"Manny," I voiced, offering up my hand. "My parents were MOTU fans, I was named after Man-e-faces."

"*Masters of the Universe*? Damn, guess it's good you weren't named Skeletor."

"In your case, they probably should have gone with Merry." In the LOTR series, the two hobbits who were best friends were Merry and Pippin. Pippin's actual name was Peregrin Took, the character Perry was named after.

Looking down I spotted her flip-flopped feet. "Glad to see you don't have hairy hobbit feet."

"And I'm pleased you don't have a giant button on your head to make it spin around as though you're possessed by an evil spirit." Still in the doorway, we stood laughing at each other.

A choir of throats cleared reminding us we weren't alone. As I turned, everyone in the room sat staring. Dawn looked pleased as punch, whatever that meant, to see us hitting it off.

"Pardon my manners. Come in, Perry." A soft whiff of perfume trailed from her as she passed, and I inhaled a deep breath of… "Strawberry?"

Flipping her hair over her shoulder, Perry grinned. "Body spray scent. You like?"

After answering, I noticed Dawn's shit-eating grin; she might have won at setting me up. "Strawberries are my favorite sweet treat."

Perry blushed, and the rest of the room fell silent as the sexual innuendo hung in the air. Never in my life had I felt so embarrassed.

Chapter Two

PERRY

ABOUT AN HOUR EARLIER

Flirting had never come easy for me. Suffering from social anxiety made it difficult for me to talk to anyone most days. But standing on the lighthouse platform, looking at this tanned god, the courage erupted inside me. I had no idea where the bravery came from. The man was out of my league. He had black hair, which appeared soft enough to run my fingers through. Silky waves left a stray strand or two falling across his forehead, accenting his dark eyes, giving him an exotic appearance. His fumbled answers to my questions left me wondering if he was as attracted to me, or just uncomfortable. When the woman approached him with the baby, I had to walk away. Although I knew they weren't together, my anxiety rose, causing a tightness in my chest and sweat to dampen my skin as panic set in.

Halfway down the walk I wanted one more peek. Turning back, I found he was watching me, so I smiled and waved before practically running back to my car. Out of the corner of my eye, as I drove out of the parking lot, I saw him sprinting toward me, but my nerve was gone.

"Hey, Perry!" Dawn called out to me as I walked into her

salon. "I'll be with you in two minutes, honey." Each month it was the same routine: haircut, manicure, and chitchat. As pathetic as it sounded, though I only saw Dawn once a month, she'd become practically my best friend. Working from home as an author had made my anxiety worse, turning me into a virtual hermit. I'd forced myself to leave the house once a week and Dawn's appointment fell on the third week of each month.

"You seem quiet today. Is everything okay?" Dawn asked as she measured the length of hair before snipping off an inch. My hair grew rather fast, but each month I only got an inch taken off, so it would never be too short. I had to stick to the regular schedule to keep my sanity in check.

"I met a guy just before I came here." Her eyes brightened. "Don't get too excited, I never even got his name. It was completely out of character for me. I saw him and felt this incredible pull to talk to him." Shrugging, careful not to affect her measurement, I added, "Maybe I'll see him again."

"Do you want to tell me about him?" Her phone rang, saving me from embarrassing myself further. Hearing the conversation, I knew she had plans to get to, so after she finished my hair, I cut out quickly leaving behind enough to cover the haircut and then some. On my way home, I calculated in my head that I'd left her a much stingier tip than usual.

Making phone calls was a huge deal for me. I pulled up Dawn's number four times before finally hitting call. Chest aching, I felt my breathing speed up, and when her boyfriend answered, I almost hung up. "Hello?" he answered for a second time.

"Hello. Um, Brady?" I hoped I had his name right. "This is Dawn's friend, Perry. Can you tell her I'm coming by? I forgot to leave her a tip earlier." I'd practiced those words in my head over and over before he answered. Hearing a male voice was something I hadn't prepared for, and a metaphorical brick sat on my chest as I wondered if I'd said anything stupid.

"Sure, babe. We'll see you soon."

I'd met Brady once at the salon when he'd come to surprise Dawn with flowers. I knew Dawn wanted to set me up with his friend, but I never could remember his name. Blind dates were pure torture for me. Finding any words to say at all was like having hot pokers stabbed into my throat while squeezing my chest in a vise. A few months back she'd asked me for a ride home, so I knew it wasn't far. I spent the entire drive over to their place worrying about what would happen when I got there. Every day I either panicked over conversations about to happen or relived past ones in my mind. The struggle was never-ending.

Standing in front of Dawn's door, I finally found the courage to knock. The person who answered knocked me back a few steps. The tanned god from the lighthouse stood with a look of shock that matched mine.

After a few minutes of flirting, I noticed the rest of the room staring at us. Suddenly I wished I was a turtle who could crawl into my shell and hide from the world, or better yet that I possessed an invisibility cloak like in *Harry Potter*.

Somehow, the seducing extrovert side of me still appeared as I flipped my hair and gave a flirty grin when Manny complimented my perfume. And then, she left. Growing discomfort forced the anxiety back out. "Here's the tip I meant to leave you, Dawn. I'll get out of your way."

Rushing toward the door, Dawn stopped me. "Please stay, Perry. There's plenty of pizza for everyone." Leaning down, she whispered, "I think it would make Manny feel like less of a fifth wheel if you stayed too." Fear of rejection tugged at me, begging me to leave and not turn back. Fighting against myself, my own worst enemy, I chose to stay.

Against my better judgment, I took a seat next to Manny. It's not that I didn't want to sit by him, there were a lot of things I wanted to do with him but not in front of all these people. A room with six people in it felt like being smothered in a crowd of a hundred to me. At times, I'd rather be in the crowd so I could fade away unnoticed.

"So, Perry, what do you do for a living?" *Oh good, there's nothing I loathe more than talking about myself.* Small talk has never been a comfort zone for me. Avoiding small intimate circles of people was a skill I'd mastered to avoid being put on the spot this way. In school, I was never the girl who raised my hand to volunteer an answer, no matter how sure I was I knew the right one.

"I'm a writer for a local paper, and I'm an author as well." Writing for the paper paid the bills more than books did. Writing books was my lifestyle, but I hadn't been successful enough to make it a full-time job. To be a best seller, you had to put yourself out there fully, and I hadn't been able to do that as much as I needed to.

"Oh, I love to read, tell me about your books," Marie asked next. Talking about my books should be easy and come naturally, but it felt even worse than talking about my private life. Most of the time, I referred people to check a website or social media for my name. It was a brush off, I know, but it was easier than attempting to talk while fumbling over my words. And for some reason, even though I wrote the books, I never could think of a decent way to explain the story without giving away everything.

"I've got nine books out currently. Mostly I enjoy writing paranormal, but the occasional romantic comedy spills out of me too. I can get your address from Dawn and send you a book if you'd like." Offering up a free book was another thing I used to save myself from talking about them more.

Appearing nervous, Dawn spoke up. "I only met Marie today. It would have to come from Manny." Dawn told me about Marie, but it had slipped my mind. She was the woman who broke Brady's heart. I'd kick my own ass right now if I could without looking crazy… *er*.

"I'll give you my email address. You can send me a link to your novels. I'd be happy to purchase them," Marie said.

Manny's hand moved from his leg to the couch, brushing mine in the process. Tingles danced across my skin with his touch. Biting my lip, I looked up at his face to see if he reacted in the same way. A half smile donned his lips, his dark eyes sparkled, and he shifted slightly closer to me. If I had more nerve, I'd ask him for his number. Hell, if I had any nerve, I might have kept eye contact, instead of dropping my gaze to my hands as I picked away at a stray cuticle.

"I need to go. Thanks for the pizza. Dawn, I'll see you in a couple of weeks." And in an instant, I was on the move again, bypassing the danger zone, taking the highway to the comfort zone instead.

Manny stood with me. "I'll walk you out." As soon as the door opened, I wanted to make a mad dash to my Jeep and speed off to the safety of my home where no one asked me uncomfortable questions or talked to me at all. I could live in the world of my characters where I felt normal and loved.

"Perry, I know we just met, but I was wondering if you'd like to have dinner with me sometime?" He appeared as nervous as I felt, which seemed odd for someone as good looking as him.

Answering with complete nonchalance, I said, "Um… sure," and shrugged as though it didn't matter one way or another. With his eyebrows furrowed and lips pursed, Manny showed genuine disappointment at my lack of enthusiasm.

"Great, maybe in a couple of weeks. I'm going out of town for the next week or so, but when I get back, I'd love to see you."

Sounding like a brush off, I casually replied, "Sure, whenever. Just give me a call." It wasn't the first time I turned a guy off, and it wouldn't be the last I was sure. Manny seemed different than any I'd met, but perhaps it was me who kept scaring men away.

One thing I noticed was he took my number but didn't give me his; classic blow off. Oh well. Life goes on. It was nice while the fantasy lasted.

* * *

The whole ride home, my inner turmoil was out of control. I relived every tiny thing I'd said since Manny and I met, both times. I picked apart his expressions and critiqued my responses to him. Torturing myself was what I did best. Social interaction had worn me out. All I wanted to do was sleep, but when I walked in the door my phone rang. I stared at the number and cringed. I'd ignored the number the last five times it had shown up on my caller ID. "Hi, Mom," I answered reluctantly. I loved my mom, both of my parents. They were as close to perfect as parents get. Talking on the phone was the part I hated. With them living at the other end of the country, in Florida, I had to answer once in a while, so they'd know I was alive.

"Hi, sweetie. Do you have a minute to talk?"

"Sure." I flopped down in my big comfy chair and pulled my legs up underneath me. "Did you get my email?" I sent emails at least once a week to check in, tell them how things were going; sometimes I sent my mom a sneak peek at one of my books.

"I did. You know I like to hear your voice too. For all I know, some maniac has you tied up and is sending the emails to keep me from knowing you need help." My mother has a little paranoia sometimes. Growing up, we were constantly protecting ourselves from the "mad rapist" who was apparently always on the run from police.

"You've been listening to that True Crime podcast again, haven't you?"

Her audible sigh spoke volumes. She'd been addicted to these two guys talking about murders in a garage. The murders weren't in a garage, but the two men running the podcast were. Every time we talked, she'd ask me if I was being safe.

"You're being safe, right?" Right on schedule as always.

"Mom, it's the guy's responsibility to bring the condoms."

"Perry," she groaned. "You know what I mean." After a brief silence, she asked, "Wait… is there a guy?"

I rolled my eyes, thankful she couldn't see me. "No guy."

"Oh." The word oozed with disappointment. Her mission in life was to see me settled down with a baby on each hip. "I hate you being alone all the time, Perry."

"I like being alone, Mom. But don't worry about me. I've been making friends here." My parents moved to Florida. I lived there for a few years with them, but a little over a year ago, I moved back to Michigan to focus on my writing career. The crowded environment of Florida was too much for my anxiety. I had a panic attack almost daily. Just before I moved, I was close to hermit status.

"Your dad and I want you to come visit. We bought season passes to Disney and would like you to join us there a few times." I did love Disney, even with the hordes of people.

"We'll see. I have two book deadlines coming up as well as a few articles I have to get written for the paper." There was also the possibility of a date with Manny. I kept that information to myself. Once I said the words out loud, I'd probably jinx any chance I had with him. Also, my mother would never stop asking me questions or wanting to know everything about him.

"Where's Dad? Can I say hi?"

"He's in the library," she groaned. I could imagine the look on her face. The library was code for my dad's bathroom time. "I'll tell him you said hello."

"Tell him I love him. And I love you too. I'll call you later."

"No, you won't. But that's okay because I'll call you. I love you, sweetie. Be careful please." I promised to be as careful as possible. Most days I was a step away from complete paranoia. I always locked my doors, stayed aware of my surroundings, and barely left the house once the sun set.

Flipping on the television, I turned on Netflix. I grabbed a blanket, chose an old favorite, *13 Going on 30,* and allowed myself to unwind for the rest of the evening.

Chapter Three

On the road with Jayce and Marie felt like old times until Constance would begin to cry. Any time her tears began to flow, I would serenade her. She'd stare up at me with her big brown eyes and grin dreamily as I grazed her cheek with my finger.

"You may have to come home with us. I've never seen her quiet so quickly!" Marie stared in awe of my baby-whispering talent. "Brown-eyed Girl" was the song I sang. It was one I used to sing to Connie when we'd speak on the phone.

"Instead of uprooting my life, how about I make you a recording you can play for her?" On the road with Marie, there were times I considered moving to Chattanooga to live near her. Starting my life over, new job, new house, new friends. Loyalty to Brady kept me in Michigan. As close as Marie and I became, nothing matched my friendship with Brady. Especially once she chose Jayce and I watched him crumble into a sobbing mess in front of me one night. Never again did I want to see such pain in his eyes.

"Deal," Marie agreed. "Even though I wouldn't mind you living closer. I promise, after this trip, I'm going to be a better friend. Plus, I'm going to want to know all about Perry."

"If there's anything to tell. She was a bit standoffish today. And when I mentioned calling her, she kind of acted casual about it." It hurt my pride a bit. Not that I expected her to fawn all over me or jump up and down as though it was the best thing ever, but a little interest would have been nice. Her lack of interest was what kept me from giving her my number in return. I knew she wouldn't call, and instead of letting it drive me crazy, I wanted to be the one holding the cards.

"Maybe she was playing it cool, not wanting to look desperate? She seemed a little shy too," Marie offered.

"She wasn't shy at the lighthouse. She was the one who approached me."

"We were doing a tourist thing. Maybe she thought she'd never see you again." Marie's idea of being helpful was making me feel worse. The thought of never seeing her again caused a pit of longing in my stomach. We'd barely met twenty-four hours ago, and I hadn't stopped thinking about her since.

It occurred to me my excuse of leaving town may have sounded like a blow off. So I decided to take a chance. Snapping a selfie with the baby, purposely including the background of the road, I typed out a text.

Me: Sending you a hello from the road. Riding in the backseat with a beautiful girl, but don't worry we're just friends. I'm looking forward to taking you on a date when I return home.

Patience had never been a virtue of mine. For the next ten minutes, I stared at my phone waiting for her to respond. Cries of hunger saved me from myself. Grabbing a bottle from Marie, I tipped it up and laughed as Constance's chubby hands cradled the bottle and sucked furiously away. Babies have it so easy and have no idea what to look forward to in life. People take care of them, love them unconditionally; they're considered adorable the fatter they are, and they don't have a care in the world.

A text came through, pulling me from my thoughts.

Perry: Looks like I have a little competition. If she doesn't manage to steal you away, I'll be looking forward to our date too.

Leaning down, I whispered to Constance, "She likes me too."

* * *

The bed-and-breakfast was exactly as Connie had described to me years ago. Being here, seeing her room, was a lot to take in. After waiting two years, her parents had started packing her room up, and they wanted us to have a chance to pick out something of hers to keep. Marie insisted I go first, so I shut the door and was alone in the world of the woman I'd loved and lost. Standing there in her bedroom brought me closer to her than I'd been since she passed away. The emotions were overwhelming. A portion of me experienced a little happiness at feeling her presence so fully here. The brief elation at being surrounded by everything Connie was short-lived as the ache to hold her again grew stronger.

Dark purple flowers filled the comforter on her bed. Seeing a bottle of her body spray on the cabinet I spritzed a little on the bed before lying on it. Soaking in her scent, I closed my eyes as I imagined her lying here with me. "You're not supposed to be in here," Connie said as she leaned over me. I grinned and pulled her into my arms, her body on top of mine. "Shh, my parents might hear us."

"I love you, chica. I don't care who hears it."

With a sweet tinkling giggle, her cheeks filled with a heated blush. Pressing her lips against mine, she moaned as my fingers traced the soft skin of her cheeks. "I love you, Manny."

"Are you going to love me if I meet someone new?"

Sad eyes, smile fading, she peered up at me through her heavy lashes. "Of course. I'll love you forever, no matter what. You deserve all the happiness in the world. And if she doesn't treat you right, I'll haunt her for revenge."

Laughing at the image of Connie trying to be mean to anyone, I replied, "I'd rather you spend time haunting me. I miss your beautiful face every day, and being here is making me miss you a million times more."

"I miss you too, but I'm always here." As she said the

word here, she placed her hand against my heart. "Don't feel guilty about moving on. You deserve happiness. I wish I could be there to give you that myself."

"Me too, chica."

Opening my eyes, I was alone once again.

It seemed odd going through Connie's things, and I wasn't sure what I wanted to keep. Stepping into her closet, I found exactly the thing sitting in a folded pile on a shelf. It was a stack of T-shirts she'd bought on her trip with Marie. Marie had sent all Connie's things home with her parents after the funeral.

She'd bought one of the shirts for me in Disney, but I asked her to hold onto it and wear it to think of me. It swallowed her whole, but the thought of it touching her skin was the closest thing to me holding her while she was on the road. The other T-shirt I chose was the one she wore the first time we were alone. It read "Just look at the flowers," a quote from our favorite show, *The Walking Dead*.

It may have only been my imaginary Connie who gave me her blessing, but I knew she wanted me to be happy. Everything in this room screamed loudly of Connie to the point I grew dizzy from the overwhelming emotions. I needed air. Since I had my keepsakes, I needed to let Marie and Jayce have a chance to say their goodbyes.

Marie and Jayce wanted to take the moment together. Connie's mom wanted to watch the baby, so I stepped onto the porch to breathe in the fresh air. Connie's dad, John, stepped onto the porch. Leaning back, he groaned as he stretched and adjusted his pants. "It's a beautiful day out.

Connie would have sat out on this porch from sunup to sundown on a day like this."

"I imagine she would be curled up on this swing with a book."

Shaking his head with a gruff chuckle, he murmured, "You knew my girl well." He stepped over and extended his hand to me. "I'm not sure if I've said it before, but thank you for taking care of my baby girl, especially in her last few months."

"Sit with me, please." Letting go of my hand, he took a seat next to me. For a moment we both stared into the distance without speaking. Enjoying the peaceful moment, I considered what it would've been like to be here visiting my in-laws. Meeting them made it easy to see where Connie's kindness came from.

"Connie loved it here. I know she took the trip because she said she needed to get away, but every time we spoke, she told me how much she missed you, Ruth, and this place. Any time she spoke of dying, I'd tell her to stop thinking so negatively, and I promised her once we'd be talking about her trip for years to come." I swallowed back the emotions threatening to spill out. In almost a whisper, I added, "I never hated not keeping a promise more."

His voice cracked with emotions as he spoke. "Once she met you, that's all she talked about when she called us. She was happier than I'd ever heard her. As much as we wanted to protect her and keep her close, I was glad to know how happy she was on the day she passed. I owe you more than just a few T-shirts for all you did for my girl."

The shirts sat in my lap and I placed my hand on them. "I'd rather have Connie back than anything else, but these are special to me." Gazing out into the field in front of the house, I sighed and closed my eyes. "Besides, having Connie for just a few months in my life was better than anything else I could ever imagine. I miss her every day. I wanted to marry her."

Her father patted my knee. "I'd have been honored to have had you as a son-in-law." Those words may sound simple, but they meant a lot to me. Connie and I talked about marriage once or twice, just in passing mostly. I told her I'd love for her dad to approve of me the way Herschel did of Glenn. We often compared life to *The Walking Dead*. Glenn was in love with Herschel's daughter Maggie. At first Herschel didn't approve of the match, but after a while he came to love Glenn like his own son. The words Herschel said to Glenn, "No man is good enough for your little girl, until one is," was a sentiment I wanted to hear about myself from John. His words were close enough for me.

After a few moments of silence, he said, "She wouldn't want you to be alone, you know? My Constance was what they call a hopeless romantic. There was nothing hopeless about her, but she loved seeing people happy. If you meet someone special, you should go for it."

"Did Marie tell you what happened before we left Michigan?" It seemed awfully convenient timing for him to mention dating.

"She might have mentioned something. Ruth asked if you'd moved on. We both would like to see you happy. We know what life without Connie is like." Again, his voice cracked with emotion. If anyone could understand my loss, it was her parents. I only wished I'd had as much time with her as they did. I felt a connection to Perry, but being here where Connie's spirit was so strong, I questioned whether I was ready for another relationship. I knew it was crazy to hang onto a memory, but it was also hard to let her go.

Chapter Four

PERRY

It had been a few days since Manny sent his text, but every time I read it, a smile appeared on my face. From the day I'd met him, he'd occupied my mind. At that moment, I had three books on my laptop with different release date goals. According to my calendar, I should've been writing my YA paranormal, but Manny's entrance into my life had sparked more of my adult writing materials. My mind was full of possibilities, sweet situations I wanted to be in with him, sexy scenarios I wished to act out.

I went with my mindset and began to write. Words flowed from my fingers with ease as I wrote mushy sentiments of love with dramatic descriptions of perfect sex. My characters spoke to each other so freely, without difficulty, that I envied the ease of their lives. The pages of the book were the only place I could say what I felt or thought without letting the world know it was truly me. Giving the characters traits and abilities that were my own, ones I kept hidden, helped lessen the burden of anxiety in having to deal with real life.

A text grabbed my attention, pulling me out of the book world.

Dawn: Would you want to grab a bite to eat?

Spontaneous plans threw my body into overdrive. Irrational fear gripped my chest at the mere thought of having to interact with someone outside my schedule. Five minutes ticked by as I stared at the damn phone taunting me. I hated this feeling inside. Most days I even hated myself because of it.

Ten deep calming breaths, and seven typed but unsent messages later, I finally responded.

Me: Sure, where do you want to meet?

While waiting for her response, I irrationally debated how mine sounded. *Was it too indifferent? Should I have added an emoticon?* My hands trembled as I glanced down at my phone, silently contemplating backing out of the plan to meet. My mouth was dry as though full of cotton. The rest of my body beaded with sweat.

Dawn: House of Flavors

There'd been a part of me hoping she'd changed her mind and tell me she had an emergency salon call, if those existed. Seeing the destination spelled out on my phone dropped a brick in my stomach. Instead of cotton, my mouth filled with saliva as nausea set in to my stomach.

Once parked, I sat in my car staring at the building as my heart raced. I closed my eyes, took a few deep breaths in through my nose, and released them from my lips. My nerves wouldn't calm easily, but it relaxed me enough for my brain to tell my legs to move.

A restaurant in town had an ice cream shop attached to it called House of Flavors. When I arrived, Dawn waved me over to the booth she occupied. "Hey, Perry! Sorry for the short notice, but Brady was supposed to meet me for lunch and had to cancel. As soon as he did, I thought of you."

"Second choice is better than fourth, right?" I said teasingly. The words stumbled out of my mouth with uncertainty. Joking around, using sarcasm, those were the masks I used to keep from crumbling from the anxiety.

Appearing embarrassed by my comment, Dawn chewed on the side of her lip. It was a talent of mine, making people speechless. I needed to suppress it a little. "Sorry, I was only kidding. I appreciate the invite."

Slipping into the booth, I glanced over the menu just in time for the waiter to appear. "What can I get you lovely women to drink?"

"Water, no lemon for me, please," I responded. Dawn ordered a soda pop.

"He's cute," I whispered as I peered back to watch him saunter away.

"Not as cute as Manny though, right?" Giving a wink, she unrolled her napkin and placed her silverware all in a row on top, a habit I had as well. "Brady spoke to him the other night, and he's looking forward to seeing you when he gets back in town."

The waiter stopped back by to take our food order, giving me a chance to process what Dawn had said about Manny being excited to see me. As soon as he walked away again, I broached the Manny subject as easily as possible, trying not to panic inside.

"Did you ask me out to talk about Manny?" It wasn't as though I didn't appreciate Dawn wanting to set me up, but it was a lot of pressure on a person. Okay, it was a lot of pressure on me.

"I asked you out because we're friends, but I know you're a little shy, and I wanted you to know Manny does like you." Being shy was always the first thought people came to with me. Social anxiety usually appeared as shyness or sometimes even uppity. If most people who had it were like me, they desperately wanted to be more outgoing, but their minds put up an exhausting fight against it. Many times, I left people thinking I was shy because it was easier than explaining the anxiety. I still relived conversations I had with people ten years ago, just to pull them apart and feel dumber every time.

"He sent me a text while he was on the road. I told him I'd see him when he gets back." The waiter dropped off our orders, and I began stabbing fries with my fork to avoid speaking for a few minutes at least. Filling my mouth with food gave Dawn the opportunity to control the conversation, and I could simply nod. Trying to use my voice during an attack of nerves was a hot mess. The words would come out jumbled, my tongue felt as though it was thick and swollen, and nothing ever sounded the way I meant it to. After stuffing my face with half the contents of my plate, I stopped. "Dawn, I do well with people I think I'll never see again. I was flirty with Manny because I didn't think anything else would come of it. Don't get me wrong, I'm flattered he is interested, and I'd be an idiot not to be interested in him after everything you've told me, but once he gets to know me, he won't want to see me again."

"Why do you say that?"

"I have… issues." Dawn's eyes widened and shifted sideways in thought. Admittedly, the phrase was a bit ominous, especially in my delivery. Closing my eyes, I took a deep breath in and released it before allowing the words to flow from my mouth. "I'm not batshit or anything. I have…" I decided just to bite the bullet and throw all the cards down. "… anxiety problems." She nodded but said nothing, so I continued. "When we do go out, I may not be able to bring myself to speak to him." Even I had to admit the words coming out of my mouth didn't come close to explaining my struggle. I needed a way to relate to her personally. "I'm not sure how to explain it without sounding like a crazy person. Do you have any phobias?"

"I'm scared of heights. Makes me a total mess. Even as low as a second story makes my stomach queasy and my head dizzy."

"Okay, that's how it feels for me to speak to someone. Even when you and I get together after not seeing each other for a few weeks, I get nervous. I debate everything I say before and after. I could recite the dictionary word for word, and I'd feel I was wrong or said something stupid. It's not logical, I know." Dawn reached across the table and placed her hand over mine. I had neglected to mention the fact I wasn't too keen on being touched either. It made my skin crawl. The weight of her hand seemed to grow heavier as it stayed atop mine. I wanted to pull it back but didn't want to hurt her feelings. Every second it stayed there, I felt my hand growing clammier.

"I get it. And I know I can't understand what you experience, but I will say Manny is one of the easiest people to talk to. It's why I've wanted to hook you guys up for so long. He's not one to easily give up on someone."

I nodded and went back to eating my lunch. Using food once again to avoid speaking, I stared down at the plate and ran a fry through ketchup while chewing another one as though they were in a tag team race and one was preparing for the hand off. Weird thoughts like those were ones I kept to myself to avoid being labeled as even weirder. Part of me wished Manny would forget he ever met me because the sheer terror resonating inside me at the prospect of talking to him again would drive me crazy. On the other hand, I couldn't stop thinking about what it would be like to kiss him.

Chapter Five

MANNY

"Can I speak to Manny alone for a minute, please?" Marie asked as she stepped out onto the porch. John stood up silently and placed his hand on Marie's shoulder momentarily before opening the door. "Let's go for a walk," she said.

Marie reached for my hand, and we walked down the stairs and out into the field in front of us. "Connie told me once this place reminded her of Herschel's farm. She wasn't kidding." The large Victorian-style house was blue instead of white, but the rest of the grounds mirrored the second season scenery of *The Walking Dead*. An old barn sat a few hundred feet from the house, surrounded by a wooden fence. "I hope that old barn isn't full of walkers." I nodded toward the structure to the right of us. All around the barn and the house was beautiful greenery and trees as far as you could see.

Marie chuckled and said, "As long as you don't go full

Shane, we can check it out." I squeezed her hand and pulled her in the direction of the barn. In the show, Shane lost his temper, opened up a barn full of walkers, and just began shooting them one by one in front of their family, who still believed they were their loved ones instead of the living dead.

"I'd never go full Shane." We stepped inside the barn, which was not full of walkers, but instead had four horses in their stalls and several bales of hay. We took a seat on a bale, and Marie laid her head on my shoulder. "Being here is a lot harder than I expected. Before, I felt like I was ready to move on, but now I don't know."

"Manny, you know Cons—"

"Would want me to be happy. I know. Everyone keeps telling me that, but I miss her so much. Some days I think I'm going crazy. I sat up in her room and could feel her there with me, Mo. I felt her lips on mine." I scrubbed my hands through my hair in frustration. "I'm losing my mind, aren't I?"

"No, I don't believe you are. You're a heartbroken man." She sat up for a moment and pulled her hair out of her face. "I'm going to tell you something I've never told anyone. And I know our situations are different, but maybe it will help you." I knew what would follow was about Brady. During our trip, Marie confided in me about a lot of things she'd never been able to talk to anyone else other than Connie about.

"When I chose Jayce, it broke my heart. I truly loved Brady. I never believed someone could love two people at the same time in the same way, until it happened to me. I mourned that loss as though he died. There were nights I imagined him being there with me. Only when I was alone, never when Jayce was with me. I love Jayce, more than anything in this world, but saying goodbye to Brady almost broke me." She glanced around as though checking for eavesdroppers nearby. "I thought I was past all that, and then I saw him with Dawn. They make a great couple, but I can't deny it hurts to see him with her. I'm glad he's happy, and I love my life, but I still miss him. When I saw him the other day, I wanted to be in his arms for just a moment."

"I had no idea, Mo." I'd noticed hints of jealousy in her eyes when she saw Brady and Dawn but never knew there was still so much yearning there.

With a sad laugh, she said, "I hide it well. I have to, especially from Jayce. I never want him to feel as though I regret choosing him, because I don't. If I'd chosen Brady, I know I'd have the same response seeing Jayce. I was meant to be with Jayce, but I never regret a moment with Brady. The only thing I regret is breaking his heart." She cleared her throat from the emotions welling up. "Your situation is different. You're going to miss Connie for probably the rest of your life, but it'll become more sporadic and will get easier."

"Just doesn't seem fair. Connie deserved to experience more in life than she did." Since Marie had shared so much with me, I felt it was my turn to share a little of my own confession. "I never believed in ghosts until Connie died. There have been moments where I feel she's with me. I know it sounds crazy."

"It doesn't. I've felt her too at times. My wedding day with Jayce. I could swear she patted my back when I cried before going out there. I wanted to marry Jayce. He's everything to me, but that day I had to say goodbye to Brady for real, and it hurt. You see why I can never tell Jayce these things, right?" No one could fault her for wanting to keep those feelings hidden. If I were Jayce, I'd question her love for me, no matter how many times she tried to convince me otherwise.

"It's no wonder we get along so well. We're both complete messes."

Marie laughed and pulled me into a hug. "I miss our talks, Manny. You're the one who talked sense into me and forced me to make my decision between Brady and Jayce. I chose Jayce because of you."

"Whoa. Never tell Brady that, please." She cringed and mouthed "sorry."

"I know what you mean though. And for the record, Brady is happy with Dawn. She's been good for him."

Marie grinned. "I agree, Manny Banany." I pulled away from her, ready to bolt, and she grabbed me in a hug, kissing my cheek and laughing. "I gotta admit, it's a catchy name."

"Do you ever wonder where we'd be right now if Connie were still alive? I mean, do you think her death affected who you chose at all?"

"Honestly?" I nodded, urging her to answer. "I think it had a lot to do with it. If she were still here, it might be the four of us living in Michigan, hanging out every weekend."

Wow. I never expected that answer from her. At most I expected an "it's possible." Instead it seemed her entire decision was based around losing Connie. "Am I a horrible person for saying that, Manny?" She placed her hand on her stomach. "I'm not glad Connie is gone, not at all. But I'm glad I made the decision I did. I wouldn't trade my family for the world."

"I know. And this stays between us. I love you, Mo." I leaned forward and placed a chaste kiss on her lips and pulled her into my arms. "Jayce is a lucky man."

"I know I am," Jayce said, smiling as he walked into the barn. "I've been looking for you two. Dinner will be ready shortly." I saw a look of uncertainty on Marie's face, probably wondering if he heard any of our talk. From the look of love in Jayce's eyes, as a man I could say without doubt he hadn't heard any of it. "Should I leave you alone?"

"No, sweetie. We're done. We were just reminiscing about Connie." Marie moved to Jayce and put her arm around his back.

"Manny, I know we haven't gotten to know each other a lot, but I know you were good for my cousin. And I appreciate the loyalty you've shown Marie. I know it can't be easy being friends with her and Brady and staying neutral."

"It's the one thing I love most about Manny. He's an amazing friend who never judges."

Jayce nodded in agreement. "I hope it hasn't been uncomfortable for you with me being here."

"No, man. I told you I want us to be friends too. What happened with you guys is in the past. Dawn makes Brady quite happy." And I saw it, the flash of hurt in Marie's eyes. She wasn't exaggerating about her feelings still being so raw. But as she leaned up to kiss Jayce, I also noticed the love in her eyes. I didn't envy her having to make that choice. "Speaking of Brady, I'm going to call him real quick and let him know we made it." I lifted my phone out of my back pocket and noticed it was sitting on a screen that read, 'Call ended.' "Well damn, it looks like I butt-dialed him, so he probably knows already."

I looked up in time to see Marie's face pale to ghostly white. She bit her lip, and her forehead creased with worry. Glancing back down at my phone, it showed the length of the call was twenty minutes, so he must have answered, but why would he have stayed on so long? *Oh shit*. I understood Marie's worried face.

"You should probably call him back," Marie suggested. "We'll head up for dinner and let them know you're on the way." She practically pulled Jayce away and rushed him out of the barn. As they were leaving, I heard him say, "What's the hurry, Mo? Are you hungry?" He laughed after the comment, so it didn't seem he suspected anything odd.

"Hey, man!" Brady answered cheerfully. "How was the trip up?"

"Pretty good. Baby C kept me company on the way. Marie got carsick a few times, but for the most part, it went fine."

"Carsick? That's weird, she never did that on her trip

that I know of." I'd forgotten Brady didn't know Marie was pregnant again. After my moment of silence, he must've figured it out. "Oh. That was quick."

I smacked myself on the head for being such an idiot. "Sorry, man, I forgot you didn't know."

"It's fine," he whispered into the phone. "It still stings a bit sometimes, but I love Dawn."

"You don't have to convince me. Look, I'm sorry I butt-dialed you before. Marie and I were talking, and I didn't realize I'd been sitting on my phone." With the way he sounded, I didn't think he'd heard us.

"I didn't even know. Must've missed it." That was odd. My phone showed the call connected, but I wasn't going to push it. Brady already got a big blow to his heart by hearing about Marie being pregnant again. "Is it hard being there for you?"

"Definitely. I miss Connie like crazy anyway, but it's ten times worse here. I got a couple of her T-shirts to bring home with me." As I spoke, I started my trek back up to the house. "I was sitting down at the barn talking to Marie about her. We're both having a hard time today. But the closure seems to be important for everyone."

"Closure is important. And Jayce?"

"He's given us some time alone. Mostly he's been taking care of baby C and spending time with his aunt and uncle." I paused a moment and said, "She's happy, Brady."

His silence spoke volumes. As much as he loved Dawn, I knew he still thought about Marie all the time. "I better go. Dawn and I have a date. I'll talk to you soon, man."

As I approached the front door, Marie stepped out on the porch, placed her hand on my chest, and gave me a nudge away from the door. She lowered her voice and asked, "Did he hear us?" Her voice trembled with fear.

"No, he didn't act like it. I know Brady well enough I'd have been able to tell. Plus, he's like you and knows he can confide in me."

"Because you won't repeat anything he's told you. Does that mean you're lying to me to protect him?" Her bottom lip trembled; she was on the brink of tears.

"I'm not lying. If he'd heard us, I'd tell you because it wouldn't be fair not to." I wrapped my arms around her and kissed the top of her head. "I told him how happy you are with Jayce. Everything is fine."

"Thank you, Manny."

Chapter Six

My latest work in progress was about a police detective who worked on the case of a woman's murder and ended up falling in love with her sister, who was a witness in the case. I'd been doing research on my computer about murder cases, enough to alert the FBI to begin monitoring me.

The murder story had become a bit intense, and even though it was created in my own mind, I'd been having trouble sleeping due to nightmares about the situation. At two in the morning, I was sitting up working on my computer, trying to lull myself back to sleep with the bright light of my laptop. However, it wasn't working. Instead I was getting several thousand words in on my book, which my publisher would love since I had a deadline rapidly approaching.

I always had several tabs open for research, Facebook, Twitter, and every other social media so I could look things up and promote as needed. An alert came up to a

Facebook notification. I went to see who else was up at this hour and saw a friend request from Manny. I hovered over the confirm button for a few minutes, stressing over whether I wanted to invite him into the world of Perry that I shared on social media. I was a lot more outgoing behind the screen than in real life, and I didn't want to give him the wrong impression of me.

Once I hit confirm, he messaged me. **Hello, beautiful lady, what's got you up at this time of night?**

He thought I was beautiful? I was thankful he couldn't witness the goofy grin on my face at that moment. **Couldn't sleep. Working on my book instead.**

Oh. Do I need to leave you alone, so you can focus?

I answered quickly, anxious to get to talk to him a little longer. **No. I could use a break. How's the trip?**

Not bad. I was having trouble sleeping too. I was thinking about you so took the chance I'd find you online. *He was thinking about me?* The thought gave me goose bumps.

Glad you did. I kept my answers short, basically because my mind was blank as to what to say. Small talk wasn't my forte. Hell, talking in general wasn't my forte. At least with typing, I didn't stumble over my words so much. At times, I fat-fingered the keys and typed odd things, but I was quick to adjust it and meticulous about making sure everything was in order before I hit Send.

I'll be home in two days. Would you like to go out on Saturday? My heart started beating faster, and I felt the sweat dampening my forehead. I hated getting so worked up over a simple question.

Sure, I typed, then backspaced and put **I'd love to,** and then backspaced again and typed **That sounds nice** and hit Send before I could change my mind again.

Great. Tell me about the book you're working on. There it was, the question I hated to answer. But I chose this line of work, so I needed to buck up. **Would you like to talk on the phone?** he asked before I could finish my answer to the first question.

Um… I have a friend staying over, so I need to keep quiet. It was a lie, but I needed warning before I spoke to someone on the phone. As silly as it sounded to people without anxiety, it's one of the hardest things to do for me.

A friend? Well, he probably thought it was a guy, and I painted myself as a lady player, or whatever you would call it. I don't think it's fair to call women whores or sluts when they sleep around, yet men are considered players, practically heroes for doing the same thing.

I lied. I have anxiety and talking on the phone makes me a nervous wreck. I couldn't believe I hit Send and let him in on that piece of me.

No problem, chica. I understand. I'm going to try and get some sleep. I'll see you in a few days. Can I pick you up or do you want to meet me?

I'll meet you. I trusted him, and Dawn spoke highly of his character, but I wanted to keep a piece of me secret for now.

Sounds good. I'll text you the place when I get back. Sleep well, sweetheart.

When he called me sweetheart it put a smile on my face. I replied, **You too**, and then we both signed off. I tried to go back to my writing, but all I could focus on was how the date would go on Saturday. I had four days to stress over one scenario after another. So much for getting some sleep.

***

Friday afternoon my anxiety levels were on high alert. For the past two days, I'd barely slept as I worried about how the date would go. Not every scenario went badly in my mind, some ended up rather dirty. The dirty ones made me more nervous as though he'd know what I'd been thinking about when he saw me. None of this was logical, but illogical was the story of my life.

I needed a friend, some social interaction to ease my mind. I showed up at the salon to see Dawn. "Hey, girl, how are you?" she greeted me. She reached to give me a hug and then stopped herself. People assumed I wasn't a hugger because I never initiated them myself. Having someone touch my hand or my shoulder made me uncomfortable. I didn't mind hugs. Being embraced was somewhat comforting, provided they didn't linger for too long. I just never knew when to give one to someone. I moved forward and gave her an awkward hug and smiled.

"I'm good. I've been in the house for a while and thought I'd get out and see a friend. Seems a bit quiet in here today. Do you mind if I hang out?"

"Not at all. Have a seat. Tomorrow's the date with Manny, right?"

I grabbed the closest seat and propped my feet up on the rails across the bottom of it. Dawn handed me a diet soda from her minifridge, and I popped the top, then took a sip. "I'm a bit nervous. He got back from his trip yesterday, didn't he? With his friend?"

Dawn frowned and nodded. "Marie. She's still here with her family for a little longer. They're at our place now."

"You don't seem so thrilled about that. I know there is history there."

Dawn gave a soft chuckle. "If it's still history."

"Are you afraid Brady still has feelings for her?"

"Maybe. From what I've heard their love affair was brief but intense. I worry about her though more than anything." The bell attached to the door rang, and we turned our heads to see Marie standing there. "Marie? What's up?"

"I was wondering if I could get a manicure? Brady says you're the best, and I need a little pampering for myself. The guys gave me a break by offering to stay with Constance." She looked back and forth between Dawn and me, and asked, "Am I interrupting? I can come back later?"

"No. Come on in and join us. Perry and I were visiting, but we can do that while I do your nails. She has a date with Manny tomorrow. She may have questions for you." Dawn winked at me. I knew part of her wanted me to help keep the conversation flowing, but I was a poor choice for that task. Dawn had been a great friend to me though, so I would make my best attempt.

"I hope it's not awkward for me to be here, based on my past with Brady," Marie said.

"It's awkward as hell, but I know it's in the past." Dawn eyed Marie curiously. I felt as though I were missing something but wasn't sure what.

Marie placed her hand over her mouth and pulled her other hand back from Dawn. "Bathroom?" she asked, muffled. Dawn pointed to the back corner, and Marie ran back there. The sound of retching followed. Dawn and I exchanged a look and a shrug.

"Oh," I commented a moment later. "I wonder if she's pregnant?"

"She is," Marie stated referring to herself in the third person as she walked out of the bathroom. "A little more than a month. The smell of the polish turned my stomach more than I expected."

"Congratulations. Brady didn't tell me you were expecting."

"Brady doesn't know. Manny does, but I thought it was weird to tell Brady." Dawn smirked. It didn't seem to me she trusted Marie much. "Did I say something wrong?" Marie asked, obviously noticing the snarky response as I did. She asked sweetly though, so I didn't believe she was a bad person. I just thought it was a weird situation. I wondered if Manny had someone in his past I needed to worry about.

"I'm sorry. It's just weird for me talking to you about Brady. He told me a lot about your time together, and it makes me a little uncomfortable I guess." I admired Dawn's honesty and tact on such a sensitive subject.

"Brady loves you. Anyone who sees you two together can see it." Marie appeared to want to reassure Dawn but also sounded hurt by the words herself. There were still feelings there if I'd read her correctly. Dawn must have noticed too because I saw worry in her features. As someone who spent their life worrying about what situation they'd get wrapped up in, I was an excellent observer of people. I hated drama though. While Marie was here, maybe I should inquire about Manny's past a little to see if there was a Marie of some kind in it.

Uncomfortable silence put my nerves on high alert. I wanted to bolt from the building and leave them to their complicated drama, but I chose to use the time to find out some information myself. "Does Manny have any ex-loves I should worry about coming back?" I offered up a little laugh to pretend as though I was only kidding, but the looks on their faces made my stomach turn. There was someone; it was obvious, and from the looks they exchanged, it was major competition for me. Staring at my phone, I considered canceling the date with Manny and avoiding any unnecessary drama before it started.

"Manny was on the trip with us because of his great love," Marie stated. The jerk asked me out just before going to see his girlfriend? "But she's no threat to you. She died two years ago." And I wish I'd never thought of him being a jerk and super glad I never said it out loud.

"Died? I don't understand."

"Her name was Constance. We called her Connie. She was my husband Jayce's cousin. A few years ago, when

I took a trip around the US and Canada, the one where I met Brady and Manny, I also met Connie. She traveled with me for most of my trip." Marie glanced over at Dawn who nodded at some unanswered question. "Brady and I were dating, and we introduced Manny to Connie, never expecting them to fall in love so quickly and strongly. Manny met us at a few spots along the way to spend time with her. They spoke on the phone daily, and Manny wanted to propose to her."

"What happened to her?" Knowing she died should've been enough; I didn't really need the details. Curiosity got the better of me. If they were willing to share, I wanted to know.

"She was born with a heart defect, and after we left Mount Rushmore, she died in her sleep in my car." Marie choked on the last few words as the tears slid from her eyes. Not only did I not avoid the uncomfortable conversation, but I made her cry, which set me on edge as well. "She was an amazing person. The two-year anniversary of her death was a few days ago. We went to Canada to see her parents and get closure." She wiped away the tears from her cheeks. "I wasn't prepared to talk about her today. I'm sorry for getting emotional."

"No. I'm sorry for asking such a personal question. Sounds like Manny was crazy about her though." Competition with a ghost was not an easy challenge to win.

"You have nothing to worry about, Perry. Manny and I had a long talk, several of them actually, and he's really looking forward to your date." She leaned forward and placed her hand on my leg, which made me stiffen at the contact. "Manny is the most amazing guy I've ever known. He's my best friend because he's the most loyal person you'll ever know, and he won't let you get away with crazy bullshit. He talks sense into you and tells you when you're being crazy. After I broke Brady's heart, he stayed friends with me even though he should've turned on me for destroying his best friend."

"Destroying is a heavy word," Dawn commented, her words full of irritation. *Yikes!* The temperature in the room dropped rapidly.

"I didn't mean it that way. Brady is crazy about you, Dawn."

Keeping her voice as steady as possible, Dawn stated, "I don't need you to tell me how Brady feels about me. We live together. I know how he feels about me. And I know how you feel about him. So, let's not talk about it anymore, please." Poor Dawn. She was on the brink of tears, and Marie sat there speechless with her mouth agape.

With only one hand painted, Marie said, "I should probably go."

Dawn wiped her eyes and stood up. "Don't be silly. I've only done one hand." Marie sat down again, and Dawn started on the other hand. The next words out of her mouth made me want to leave before things got heated again. "I picked up Brady's phone the other day and heard you and Manny talking. It was obvious it was a butt-dial, and I started to hang up, but something caught my attention."

"Oh" was all Marie said, but her face told me a much

longer story. Something had been said in that conversation that should have stayed between Manny and Marie. "How much did you hear?"

"Enough to know you're still in love with Brady."

"But I'm not. I mean, I'll always care for Brady, that's true, but I love my husband and don't want to be with Brady. You belong together. I can see how happy you make him. And I'm not trying to act as though I know him better than you. It's just sometimes an outsider can see things clearer. You two have already been together longer than he and I were." Marie sounded genuine, and it seemed Dawn was trying to take her words to heart. Me? I was looking for the nearest exit, wondering how rude it would be to run out of here.

"I met him shortly after you two broke up. I saw the pain when he spoke of you. I know part of him still loves you and always will. It just hurt hearing you say the same thing."

Marie placed her free hand on her stomach. "Jayce, Constance, and this little one, they're my life now. Brady and I will never be together again. We were never meant to be." The bell rang in the middle of Marie's little speech, but she didn't turn around until she noticed Dawn's face. Marie turned to see Brady looking shell-shocked and Jayce's jaw tensed in frustration.

"Shit." Marie stood up with one and a half hands painted. "I'm going to go. I keep saying all the wrong things." Brady reached out for Marie, stopping her before she got to the door.

"You're right. We weren't. I was meant to be with Dawn.

You didn't say anything wrong. Please stay." Brady's eyes pleaded with her. As an author, it appeared to be a look of longing and want, and his words didn't match his expression.

Dawn seemed happy with what she heard, which was important. Manny stepped in behind Jayce, holding Constance in his arms. He glanced around the room. "Wow. What did I miss?"

His confusion turned into a smile when his eyes landed on me. Goose bumps danced across my skin. No one had ever looked so happy to see me, and it gave me butterflies. "Hey, Perry," he said as he sauntered over, still cuddling the baby girl. "I didn't expect to run into you. We're still on for tomorrow, right?"

"Yep," I said confidently. "I'm looking forward to it." Seeing the way his smile brightened and his eyes lit up, I grasped the fact I'd been very nonchalant about the date until this moment. The baby reached out and lunged toward me. "Oh," I said as I caught her, and Manny released her into my arms.

"She must like you because she doesn't usually go to people so easily." With his index finger, he gently stroked her cheek, and she cooed against his hand. "Constance, this is my friend Perry."

"Constance?" I hadn't considered her name before. The baby was named after the love of his life? He simply nodded and continued playing with her. He stood so close I couldn't focus on the baby. Instead I focused on the subtle smell of his cologne invading my nose. His arm brushed against mine, and I noticed his muscles flexed. My eyes moved to his chest, which I could tell was quite defined—even beneath his somewhat loose T-shirt.

"She's beautiful," I commented once I found my voice again.

"Thank you," Marie replied. "We should probably get on the road. I think we've overstayed our welcome," she whispered to Manny who appeared heartbroken.

"I thought you were staying a little longer?" he asked.

"I think it's causing issues with Brady and Dawn, and I don't want to hurt him any more than I have." She wrapped her arms around Manny. "I love you. I promise to see you again soon." Marie reached for Constance who eagerly went to her mom. "And this little girl is going to miss her Uncle Manny so much. You'll have to come down and see us when…"

"He knows," Manny whispered. Marie frowned and bit her lip as she looked back at Brady. He spotted her and exchanged a sad smile with her. "He's good, Mo."

"I should go." I felt like an intruder standing here listening to this conversation. "I'll see you tomorrow, Manny."

"I'm looking forward to it." He winked after repeating my earlier sentiment. "I'll see you at the restaurant around six." I quickly waved goodbye to everyone and scurried out the door. I glanced back as I left and saw the uncomfortable-looking group of people trying to talk. There seemed to be a lot of drama surrounding that group of friends, and I wasn't sure I was built for dealing with it.

Chapter Seven

MANNY

First date disaster was putting it nicely. Maybe I expected every first date to be like it was with Connie. When we met, it was as though I were talking to someone I'd known my entire life. With Perry it was… different.

Perry had insisted we meet at the restaurant instead of me picking her up, which was fine since we were technically strangers. Dawn had warned me she was quirky, so I didn't want to push things. And Perry had told me herself she had some anxiety; I just wasn't sure the extent of it.

When I arrived at the Ludington Pub, a place I frequented, I quickly spotted Perry sitting at the bar having a pink fizzy drink. Careful not to startle her, I stepped to her right and leaned down. "Hey, stranger, do you want to grab a table?"

Barely looking up, she replied, "Nope, I'm cool here." Not a terrible start, I could gaze at her longingly through the mirror if I wanted, if she looked up. "Did you get a chance to look over the menu?"

She shrugged and gave a curt reply. "A little."

"Mind if I order us some appetizers? The food here is fantastic." Maybe food was the way to get her to open up more. She simply shrugged again and nodded.

Flagging down the bartender, I ordered. "I'd like Naked Wing Dings and Hot Pepper Cheese balls and an ice-cold Corona with a lime." Turning to Perry, I asked, "Would you like to order another drink? What is that?"

"Shirley Temple. I probably need something stronger to get through this though." Well damn, I didn't realize it took drinking to get through a date with me. Strike one on things going smoothly.

"Give the woman a shot of something, I suppose."

"Strongest shot you have, please." Strike two, in my opinion. Same reasoning but adding the "strongest you've got" cut deep to my balls.

"Are you sure you want to be here tonight? Did Dawn force you to say yes?"

"No?" she asked like it was a question. Was I supposed to know the answer?

"If she did, I'll let you off the hook." The bartender returned before she could respond, but I noticed in the mirror, she seemed to be glancing around in need of escape. *Why not torture myself more?* I kept talking. "So, you write, correct?"

"Correct." And one word was all she gave me. I wished I'd searched her books, so I could know more about what to mention to get her talking.

"What genre?"

"Different ones."

"Such as…" Talking to this girl was like pulling teeth. But something about her made me want to keep drilling away, which sounded much dirtier than I meant.

"Paranormal romance, contemporary romance, erotica."

"Erotica? Really?"

Rolling her eyes, she replied, "Yes, so now if I tell you I went to Catholic school all my life, are you going to want to see the uniform too?" Normally I'd have made a comment trying to be cute and flirty, but instead, I sat quietly feeling disappointed at how things were going.

My balls and wings arrived saving my actual balls from the beating they seemed to be taking. Popping a hot pepper ball in my mouth, I chased it with a large sip of Corona, after squeezing lime juice in it first.

"First date?" the bartender asked me when she delivered our food.

Perry kept her head down, so I answered instead, "I think I'm blowing it."

"Sweetie, if she blows it with you, I'm available." Caressing my hand with her slightly calloused one, I cringed a bit when she smiled to show me her blackened teeth. I'm not a picky guy, but hygiene, especially toothpaste, was too easy to come by to let your teeth get that bad.

"Perry, perhaps you'd like to go somewhere else?"

"I think I want to go home. I'm sorry, Manny. I'll pay for my share." And before I could say anything, she plopped a twenty on the bar and strolled out.

"Fucked that up somehow," I mumbled to myself.

"Another one, please." I pointed to my beer and said, "And a cheeseburger, medium, I like it to moo a little at me, with an order of fries."

"Sure thing, sexy," the bartender cooed. Picking up the phone, I texted Dawn to let her know how smooth my moves were. And then I texted Marie to complain about my sucktitude. My phone rang with a call from Marie.

"Did you call to make fun of me?"

"No. I called to tell you to go after her. Sitting with Perry, I noticed a few telltale signs I'd seen before in one of my aunts. She seems to have some issues with anxiety of some form. Her mannerisms, her short speech, the fidgeting she did the entire time we were there, all point to it. I've done research on this stuff before. We used to think my aunt was bitchy or antisocial, but it was something she couldn't control." Marie paused. "In a way it's like a paranoia of sorts. No matter what you say, her brain is picking up different vibes from you and assuming you don't like her."

"When I talked to her on Facebook, she told me she had anxiety. Admittedly I didn't really know what she meant exactly. Tell me how to convince her I do like her?"

"Patience, perseverance, presentation, a bunch of P words. Just don't be a pervert. Although I have heard that sometimes people who are introverts are freaky in bed."

"Really, Mo? Let's not go there yet. I'd like the girl to talk to me first." Sex was important to me—it's important to every guy—but it wasn't everything. Connie and I had some of the best sex I've ever experienced, but it wasn't what I missed about her. Our talks, late nights on the phone while she traveled, the way she whispered "I love you" the first time she said it, the cute way she tucked her hair behind her ear and blushed when I complimented her. In her last letter to me, she asked me to find love again and told me I may have to work for it but to never give up when I met the person, stating I'd know it when I saw her. When I saw Perry the first time, those words ran through my mind.

"Give it some thought, Manny. If she seems worth the trouble, then call her."

Downing the last sip of beer, I left money on the bar and headed out to my car. Across the street, I spotted Perry sitting in her Jeep with her head resting on the steering wheel.

Lightly rapping my knuckles on the driver's side window to get her attention, she jumped in surprise. While she searched for the window button, I noticed her face was puffy and wet. She'd been sitting outside crying for the last twenty minutes?

"Did something happen?" I asked her once the window was down. "Why are you crying, chica?"

Swiping her thumbs across her cheeks, she tried to get rid of any evidence. "I'm sorry about earlier, Manny. I think you're a great guy, and you deserve someone with less baggage than me."

"How about you let me decide what I deserve or want? Can I join you in the car?" Perry reached over to unlock the door, essentially inviting me into the car with her. I might have given up on her before with all her crazy anxiety moments, but a little voice in my head told me she was worth it. Stumbling forward, I mumbled, "I got it." I could swear I'd been given a little shove to get moving.

I never believed in a hereafter until Connie came into my life. When she passed, I started having weird sensations and a feeling of never being alone. After my first drunken one-night stand, I swear I even felt a slap upside my head acknowledging the crappy choice I'd made. Some people would probably say it was just my imagination, and it very well may have been. Still, there was a part of me happy to believe Connie was still nearby.

"Let's talk. Tell me whatever you want to tell me and leave out anything you feel you're not ready to share."

Chapter Eight

PERRY

Arriving at the bar earlier, I wanted to throw up I was so nervous about one-on-one time with Manny. The thought of eating anything made me want to puke. I ordered a Shirley Temple because it has lemon-lime soda in it to pacify my stomach. From the time Manny showed up, my chance at a second date went from sixty to zero in a matter of seconds.

Walking out of the bar, I had every intention of driving away and not looking back. Instead, my emotions betrayed me. My body was shaking so much from anxiety, my fingers couldn't turn the key to start the ignition. Because my eyes were welling with tears, the view through the windshield was unclear. Hugging my steering wheel, I sat there and cried until my head hurt.

Startled by knocking, I peered up into the beautiful brown eyes of the caramel-skinned, muscular god I'd been dreaming of seeing again. The same one I expected to never see after walking out on him like a crazy person in the middle of our date.

Gleaming white teeth greeted me until he saw my face and his smile faded away. This man must love torturing himself to want to talk to me again.

Was I ready to tell him my innermost personality secrets? Could anyone handle hearing all the traits of mine with this anxiety issue? Dealing with people was one of the most difficult things to endure on a daily basis. Sweaty palms, shaking hands, stuttering speech, sometimes the complete inability to speak, it all came with meeting new people or crowds or just interacting with someone new one-on-one. Second dates were almost nonexistent for me.

If I could make Manny understand all the craziness and want a second date, then we might have a decent shot. The few friends I had were people who pushed hard enough to get me to speak to them. No matter how little information I gave Dawn, she was always able to pry more out of me. Eventually I told her most of my life story. Once I started talking, sometimes I couldn't shut up.

Sweet, musky cologne filled my car, and I wanted to bathe in it. As shaky as my hands were, I wanted to run them over his smooth muscles, comb my fingers through his thick, black hair, and I wanted to taste the sweetness of those pale pink, plump lips of his.

Lost in fantasy, I forgot to speak. It must have been interpreted as nervousness because Manny patiently waited for me to say something. His patience was important, because without it, we'd never have even a remote chance.

"Have you ever known anyone with social anxiety?" I asked timidly, choking on the word social making it sound more like slushal, which wasn't a word.

"Not personally, but my friend Marie was telling me about it." Great, so he'd been telling people how screwed up I am, enough that his friend was able to diagnose me.

"What did she tell you?" I was almost afraid to ask because many times people missed the most important aspects. When he relayed it all to me though, I was surprised to find she hit everything on the dot.

Manny surprised me by saying, "I'd like a shot at another date." Immediately my mind began going over worst-case scenarios of another date. *How bad would I screw that one up? How fast could I make this man run? Is this a pity date?* Admittedly, I wanted to smack sense into myself for having these thoughts so frequently; I knew other people wanted to smack me at times too.

"That… yeah… it's good. I mean, I'd like to." I laid my forehead on the steering wheel and groaned in frustration. Manny placed his hand on my hair and made soothing strokes. When people touched me, I tensed up and panic set in. Nothing happened when Manny touched me, well nothing negative. My body responded to him in a calming way. The panic in my chest lessened.

Lifting my head, I turned to look at him in awe. "How do you have this effect on me?"

He smiled. "A good one, I hope?"

"Different, but definitely good."

Chapter Nine

MANNY

"I know you didn't feel comfortable in the crowded bar. Would it be easier for you if I pick us up an order and we go back to my place?" Her eyes widened in shock with assumption. "I didn't mean… what about if I grab us a couple of burgers and we eat in the back of my truck?" Inside I'd ordered a burger but never got around to eating it since I'd been on the phone with Marie.

"That sounds nice. I have a blanket." Perry reached behind the seat and grabbed a large, fuzzy blanket with Rob Pattinson as a sparkly vampire. She blushed and said, "I was a big Twihard. Don't judge me." I chuckled when she winked at me and giggled a little. She was kind of adorable.

While she went to spread the blanket out in the bed of my truck, I ran inside to place our orders. They told me it would be a few minutes, so I waited by the window watching her. Not in a creepy way but to make sure she didn't panic and try to leave again.

Her emotions seemed to be all over the place. One moment she'd be relaxing with a smile soaking in the sun, and the next she was glancing around looking panicked. I knew it was all part of the anxiety.

"Sir, your order is ready." I turned to see a young girl holding up two bags of food for me. She looked exactly like Connie at first view. As I walked closer to her, I saw the resemblance wasn't as precise as I initially thought. Somehow it felt like another sign I was doing the right thing by pursuing this thing with Perry.

At the truck, Perry was standing up and lifting the blanket off the bed. She paused when she saw me and set it back down. "Everything okay?"

"I thought you changed your mind," she said. Damn, this woman had serious abandonment issues. I needed to know more about what caused all this uncertainty in her life. "Burgers and fries are fresh, so it took a moment. I hope you're hungry. It looks like they overloaded us with fries."

Perry took the drinks from me and then the food, so I could lift myself up. The truck groaned under my weight as I stepped inside to join her.

She unwrapped her burger and wrapped her lips fully around the half pounder with all the toppings on a large bun. I had to admit it was pretty hot to watch. I loved a girl who wasn't afraid to eat. Connie was that way. I shook the thought from my mind. I had to quit thinking about her and move forward. Not everyone needed to measure up to her, but mostly I compared her often because she had everything I'd never known I wanted in a partner.

"Are you thinking about her?" she asked timidly.

My head snapped up because I didn't know how she could possibly have guessed. "Who?" I asked, unsure of what she knew.

"Dawn said her name was Constance. Is that right?"

"Oh. Yeah. She told you about her?"

"A little. She said you hadn't dated since she passed. She told me how hard it was on you and still is. I see what she means now. Is this uncomfortable?" She put a fry in her mouth and bit down, chewing almost nervously it seemed, instead of savoring it.

"Not at all. Connie was important to me, I won't deny that, but she's gone. It's been two years, so I have an easier time talking about her than I used to. I'll admit I was thinking about her just now, but not in the way you think."

"What does that mean?" She ran her french fry through the ketchup dripping off her burger.

"You may think I'm crazy when I tell you this." As soon as the words left my mouth, she doubled over in laughter. "What's funny?"

"You assume I have room to think anyone is crazy based on the way I've acted since we met."

"There's nothing crazy about you, Perry. I think you're sweet, and I want you to have more confidence in yourself and more confidence in my feelings toward you." Her eyes widened, possibly in fear. Now she probably thought the crazy man (me) was trying to confess his love for her. "By feelings, I mean I like you. I want to get to know you better, and if you're up for it I want more dates like this one."

"You don't mind eating in the back of the truck with me, instead of inside the nice restaurant?" She tilted her head in question.

"I'm an outdoorsy guy anyway, so this is a much better date in my opinion. Plus, we don't have an audience. I certainly don't need one." Life in the spotlight had never been my idea of a good time. I enjoyed my privacy.

When I looked up, she had ketchup on the side of her mouth. The sweet smile she gave me said she was clueless it was there. I didn't want to make a big deal about it, potentially embarrassing her in the process. I took a napkin and dabbed at her face. She froze in place like a scared bird when I touched her.

"I'm sorry. I shouldn't have assumed that was okay." Instead of getting upset, she leaned forward and pressed her lips against mine. It was my turn to freeze in place with my eyes wide open in shock.

Her soft lips moved against mine at first by themselves, and once my brain registered what was happening, I joined in. Though it felt like several minutes, I'm pretty sure it was only a second or two because she didn't run away from me with humiliation.

Perry could kiss. And not to sound like a girl, but the kiss made my toes tingle. In a manlier description, I'd say it made me hard, but the moment was sweet, and I didn't want to push things.

Hardness was definitely becoming an issue though. She sat back and smiled sheepishly at me. "That was a nice surprise" was the only thing I could say.

"I've never done that before. It's weird. It's like something else was pushing me to kiss you." I couldn't help the grin on my face. *Connie, you little matchmaker.*

"I have the distinct feeling we might have a bit of a cupid on our side." I winked, and her eyebrows crinkled with curiosity. I probably sounded like a whack-a-doodle, but truthfully, I didn't care as long as she wasn't scared away.

And my whack-a-doodle glory didn't seem to offend because she smiled. Sitting back, she seemed more relaxed. Being there under the stars with her was peaceful. While we quietly ate, I kept stealing glances at her. Watching her movements, the little fidgets she had, I didn't compare them to anyone. They were uniquely Perry. With one hand, she continued putting french fries in her mouth, one at a time, while the other hand tugged on the strand of hair hanging down in front of her eyes.

Every few minutes, she'd lick her lips. And like clockwork, she would scratch her nose as though she had a tickle. As weird as it sounded, I could have sat and watched her little quirks for a while. When she peered up at me, I tried to pretend I hadn't been staring.

"Are you ready to call it a day, or would you like to take this elsewhere?" I hoped I wasn't being too forward.

"I'd like to go back to your place and continue what we started, but I think it's best we save something for the second date."

I grinned. "Ah, so there will be a second date?" She nodded, and I pumped my fist in the air and exclaimed,

"Yes!" She giggled at my delightful (if I do say so myself) display of excitement.

"I better head home before I decide to ease on into date two. Can I call you tomorrow?" The question came out before I remembered how she felt about talking on the phone.

"Um… sure." Before knowing a little more about anxiety, I would've taken her uncertainty to mean she didn't want to talk to me.

"No pressure, sweetheart. If you would rather wait until our next date, we can do that. Or we could talk through text or private message if you prefer." When we chatted while I was in Canada, I picked up on the fact she was much more vocal, so to speak. Behind a screen, a cage to protect her emotions, seemed to be the most comfortable way for her to be herself. I wanted to know the real Perry, and I felt she was worth the extra effort.

"Sounds great. Thanks, Manny, for being so understanding." Placing a sweet kiss on my cheek, she stood up, and I jumped up to follow her.

"Hold up," I said just before she climbed out. I stepped down onto the ground first and asked, "May I?" She nodded. I placed my hands on her hips, and she squealed as I lifted her from the truck. Standing only inches apart, I leaned in to taste her lips one more time. She tasted like strawberries, which was the flavor of her lip gloss I saw in the cab of her Jeep at the "official" beginning of our date.

"Can we make an agreement?"

"What type of agreement?" Skepticism was a great

talent of hers.

"A signal. If I'm making you happy, you fidget with your fingers and run your hand over your earring." I smirked at the confused look on her face when she realized she'd been doing those exact motions.

"Funny." She blushed, settling her hands into mine. "Maybe the signal should be, I'll tell you if I don't want to see you anymore?"

"Sounds simple enough. And I promise to respect you and leave you alone if you give me the signal. After tonight, I hope you don't say it. See you soon, pretty lady." I made sure she got in her Jeep and drove off before I went back to my truck. As if I had radar on me, a text from Brady came through.

Brady: How was the date?

Me: Let me guess, Dawn wanted you to check?

Brady: Of course. Have I ever asked you about a date before? It's not what guys do, man.

Manny: We're not typical guys, but I get what you mean.

Brady: You're killing me, man…

I knew the longer I waited to answer, the more Dawn would bug him about what I said. I set the phone on the seat next to me and started my drive home. The texts came in a few minutes apart, but I didn't check them. Don't text and drive; I lived by that with no exceptions.

When I arrived home, I had three messages from Brady calling me every name in the book and telling me what a douche bag I was. I dialed his number, and when he picked up the phone, he stated, "Douche canoe. You know she's been bugging the hell out of me wanting to know intimate details of your date."

"Perv. Why didn't she call Perry?"

"You know how Perry is about that stuff. I—" Brady started.

"Manny, I need to know how it went, please." Dawn's sweet voice replaced Brady's snarky one. I chuckled at how manipulative she sounded with her wooing tones. "I baked some fresh chocolate chip cookies. Why don't you come by and have some with vanilla bean ice cream?"

"You're a mean temptress, Dawn. I'll be right over. Give me ten minutes. I'm taking the bike." With the town being as small as it was, I often rode my bicycle to get in a little fresh air and exercise.

Brady and Dawn lived only a few miles from my house, so it didn't take me long to get there. The faint smell of chocolate wafted through the door as I stood ready to knock. Dawn whipped the door open holding a plate full of delicious-smelling cookies.

"Did you put pecans in them?"

"Yep, just how you like them." She smiled her manipulative smile as I grabbed a cookie and bit down into the soft, gooey middle.

"You really love me, don't you?" She winked and tugged me inside. "Calm your—"

"If you say my tits, I'm going to smack you upside the head."

I raised my hands in surrender and finished with "self"

instead of "tits" as I originally planned.

When Brady met Dawn, I was happy for him finding someone, but we didn't immediately click like I had with Marie. After a few months of their dating, Brady asked me to join them for a weekend getaway, and one night she and I stayed up having a late-night chat.

The topic had been none other than Marie. Brady had whispered her name in his sleep, and they got into a fight over it. She told him she wanted to sleep on the couch for the night and found me curled up with a book.

Letting go had been hard for Brady, but when he told me he'd fallen in love with Dawn, I believed him. And I relayed that information to her. I should have been a psychologist for all the advice I'd given the women in my life.

My advice seemed to have gone over well for most, but with Marie, it ended up breaking my best friend's spirit for a while. In the end, I believed they were better off apart. Jayce and Marie had a connection Brady wouldn't have been able to come between, and it would've ended badly eventually.

Dawn placed a bowl with two scoops of vanilla bean ice cream in front of me and edged the sides with fresh cookies. "You don't have to bribe me, Dawny Bear."

Her forehead creased, and her nose wrinkled in disgust. "Dawny Bear?"

"I'm working on getting you a nickname as annoying as Manny Banany. I'm not content with that one, though the look on your face was priceless." She swatted my arm playfully and then kissed my cheek. "You're lucky I like you."

I finally gave in to her demands and spilled all the dirty details about the date with Perry. I kept the personal stuff to myself out of respect for Perry's privacy but told about the awkwardness at the beginning and how in the end it all worked out nicely.

Dawn squealed with delight and clapped. "I knew you two would hit it off."

"What gave you the impression we would exactly?" The moment I met Perry I knew I wanted to know more, but I wasn't sure how Dawn thought we'd make such an amazing match.

"She's so quiet and shy. I knew that if anyone would take the time to break down her walls. it would be you. You're a patient guy, Manny. And you're a romantic above anything else."

"The walls were practically built from vibranium. It was hard to even make a dent." I didn't think before I mentioned the next detail. "If it hadn't been for Marie's advice, I might have given up on her after she walked out of the bar."

Dawn's excitement faded a little at the mention of Marie's name. "What do you mean?"

"I called to talk to her after Perry walked out, and she told me her impression from when they spoke was that she would need a little extra attention to open up."

"Marie's pretty intuitive when it comes to people," Brady commented.

Dawn laughed. "This is the same woman who didn't know her best friend was in love with her for how many years?"

Brady didn't get offended by the question at all. Instead we all had a laugh about it because she had a valid point.

"In all honesty, Jayce didn't know he had feelings for Marie either. It was a mutual ignorance of sorts." Laughing at my friend's expense seemed wrong to me so I needed to defend her a little to make up for it.

"Touché," Dawn replied. "Even though I think you should've called me since I've known Perry longer, I appreciate Marie's interference in getting you two together. I guess we have something in common after all." Brady and I exchanged a look that didn't go unnoticed by her. "Okay, so *more* than one thing." Another nice moment of laughter erupted between the three of us.

"I have a fun idea," Dawn suddenly exclaimed, making me nervous.

"If you say double date, I'm out." She frowned, and I knew my assumption was correct. "No offense, but let's wait until she and I have had a few more dates. Let me get to a point where she feels comfortable with me before bringing in extra bodies to ramp up her anxiety."

"That's fair. Although technically, she's already comfortable with me." Dawn must have noticed my annoyance with her response, so she raised her shoulders in surrender. "Just saying. After three or four dates though, I would like all of us to go out at least once. I think it will be good for her to get to know more people in town."

My current priority was for Perry to be more comfortable with me; we could work with the rest of society later.

Chapter Ten

I woke up in a sweat after a vivid dream about Manny. Our kiss was still fresh in my mind, and I wanted more. More kissing, more touching, more Manny. My entire body tingled each time I thought of him.

I'd dated a little when I was living in Florida, but when I moved to a small town, thinking it would help my apprehension lessen, I found it hard to meet anyone. Flirting had never been one of my strengths. Society always says women talk too much, but most of the men I've gone on dates with seemed turned off when I didn't say much. Manny definitely wasn't most men.

My anxiety hadn't been cured by the move, but it was getting a little better recently. I believed Dawn, and Manny, were to thank for it.

My publishing company had been pushing me to do some signings. My books were selling at a slow rate, but I definitely had a following of loyal fans. The thought of traveling on my own scared me to death. Being alone I could handle, but the longer I spent by myself, the harder it was to be around people again.

When I checked my email, I had an alert for an invitation to a convention in Michigan only a few hours away. Frankenmuth, Michigan, was a small tourist town about three hours from Ludington. The convention was in its third year, and I'd heard great things about it but had never been. There were authors I followed on Facebook who went every year, and it always looked like everyone who attended became the best of friends because of it.

My publisher was copied on the email, and she had replied to me, stating she wanted me there, no exceptions because it was close by. Luckily, I had several months to prepare myself emotionally for it.

Hitting the reply button, I reluctantly typed (then deleted, retyped, repeat) until I was satisfied with the answer I gave, which was I would work on my budget and see if I could fit it in.

Almost instantaneously I received an email from my publisher that stated, "We're booking a half table for you, and we will cover the cost on this one."

Shit. There went my budget idea. And a half table meant I'd sit closely with another author, most likely a stranger who would be more outgoing than I ever could have been.

A moment later, I received an email that welcomed me to the book event along with my tickets for the event, which included my table, lunch, and a ball. *Crap.* A dance of all things? Transported back to high school in an instant, I saw myself walking the halls spotting the posters for the dance, seeing all the happy couples buying tickets, and I remembered that on those nights, I sat at home wondering what it would be like to be there with whoever my current crush was at the time, whatever real or fictional male brightened my fantasies.

On the bright side, if Manny and I worked out, I could ask him to go with me. After that many months together, if we got there, it wouldn't be so weird to go on a trip with him. Perhaps I could even invite Brady and Dawn along, and we could have a couples' getaway.

Whoa. Back up, Perry. You're getting ahead of yourself as always. You had one date with Manny, shared a fabulous make-out session, and he asked you out for a second. Take one thing at a time before you end up overwhelmed.

The event coordinator was an author who I'd heard was very kind, so it could turn out to be a step forward in my career to put myself out there in the public eye.

The theme this year was gods and goddesses with full-on togas. The image of Manny in a toga with nothing underneath made me reach over and turn the fan on next to me.

Next time I slept, I wouldn't be surprised if the toga made an appearance on, or off, Manny in my dreams. According to my alarm clock, morning was rapidly approaching. My inbox went from sixty unread messages to two. At least I made some progress there. My book, however, stayed steadily at twenty-five thousand words. With a deadline of two months looming for this one, I had to get to sixty thousand words at least for it to be released as a full novel.

Most books I knocked out in two months flat. I'd been working on this one for six now. My mindset had been all over the place, and I'd been unable to focus enough for a story to spill forth.

The hero hadn't even kissed the heroine yet. They'd had their meet cute, but nothing more. Come to think of it, there had been a lot of filler in there for them, which meant I'd probably be cutting my word count some.

Most normal people would be getting up and preparing for a day out of the house but not me. I'd decided to lie back down and try to get a little shut eye since I'd slept so horribly the night before.

Three hours later, I gave up on trying to get a full night's sleep and made the bold choice to go out in public.

The first place I stopped was the diner on main street to grab some breakfast. The moment I walked in, I cringed at hearing my name called out. "Hey, Perry, how's it going?"

"Brady, good to see you." Have I mentioned I suck at small talk? Saying it was good to see someone always sounded like a lie coming from my lips because I hated running into anyone.

"You too." He looked as uncomfortable as I knew I was. "I know you aren't a fan of crowds, but…" and the rest of the sentence went to the back of my mind as I cringed, hating when people voiced what I didn't like. It was just their way of telling me I didn't hide my insecurities as hard as I tried to. My brain registered the rest of his comment as he asked, "Dawn wants to do a double date. Manny told her he wanted to wait until you're more comfortable with him. So, if I buy tickets for a concert in two months, do you think you'd be interested? There's a heavy metal band coming to town the three of us enjoy, and I wanted to surprise Dawn. If you're not comfortable with it—"

Placing my palm straight in front of my face, I stopped his ramble. "Sounds fun. As long as you let me pay for my ticket in case Manny doesn't want to continue dating, so you don't lose money."

Brady grinned. "You may not want to continue dating Manny. He's a bit of a tool sometimes." I laughed at his facetious comment. From the time spent with Manny and everything Dawn had told me, I knew he wasn't being serious.

I reached into my wallet and grabbed one of my author business cards. At home, I had almost a thousand going unused because I hated talking about myself, so I rarely ever gave them out.

"This has my email information on it. Send me the link, and I will purchase my ticket."

"Let me get them and you can pay me back, that way we can all sit together. I want to get her front row seats."

"Oh." Front row sounded slightly out of budget for me, and Brady seemed to pick up on it.

"What if you pay me the cost of a regular ticket and I cover the upgrade to front row?" Before I could argue he added," "I know you're worried about this thing with Manny not working out, but the guy has been my best friend for years, and I gotta tell you I've only seen him so excited about one other girl. Besides that, he's someone who can be friends with his ex if things don't work out."

"How does that work for you and Marie? Being friends, I mean?" *Open mouth insert foot, Perry. Nice job.*

"At first it sucked, but it's gotten easier to see her with Jayce, and I have Dawn now."

"How does Dawn cope with it?" *Why could I not quit speaking?*

"I'm guessing you mean because of the little conversation just before Marie left?"

The more personal the conversation got, the more uncomfortable I felt. "You know, forget I asked. I need to grab breakfast; my blood sugar is low, and I tend to ramble." Not totally true, but not a complete lie either.

"I'll email you about the concert, Perry. Bye now." Brady waved as he walked out the door. In my head, I ran through scenarios of what he would say to Manny about our encounter. I hated my head for having such a crazy imagination, then again it did add to my livelihood as an author.

The girl at the counter watched Brady leave and exchanged a grin with her coworker. "He's taken," I offered up to them, and they both rolled their eyes at me. Most likely they both assumed I had staked my claim to him, but I was simply defending my friend Dawn. New friends were hard for me to find, but I was fiercely loyal to those in my life.

Placing my order was fun as the girl rolled her eyes with every word I spoke. Thankfully the computer was sending the information to the cook, and I didn't think there was a button for spitting in the food. I hoped there wasn't at least.

Turning around, I bumped straight into the person behind me. "Sorry," I mumbled as I brushed past.

I grabbed my tray from the counter and found a seat in the farthest corner of the restaurant. A text came through just as I took the first bite.

Manny: Are you busy tomorrow night?

Me: Nope.

Manny: Excellent. Can I pick you up this time or would you still prefer to meet?

Me: You can pick me up. 7?

Manny: Perfect! Send me your address.

After texting him my address, I no longer had an appetite. The nerves had stolen away my hunger.

***

Date two, take two. Manny arrived at my house a few minutes before seven. I heard the car door shut and watched him work through his nerves, which helped ease mine. Knowing he was just as nervous as me made it easier to be myself. He shook his fisted hands and jumped around like a fighter preparing for his bout.

When he knocked, I was standing right next to the door, but I counted to ten, took a few deep breaths and shook off my own worries before opening the door.

"Hey," we said at the same time.

"Do you want to come in for a minute?" I invited,

secretly hoping he'd want to stay in for the night.

"I have a full night planned if you're up for it." A full night probably meant lots of people around. The look of excitement in his eyes was hard to ignore, so I swallowed my insecurities and grabbed my jacket before closing the door.

Manny opened the car door for me, and I slipped inside and watched him run around to the driver's seat. "Where are we going first?"

"It's a surprise." He would quickly learn I hated surprises. They gave me no room to prepare for what might happen.

Silently dreading what was to come, unable to overthink the very outcome of each situation, I stared out the window.

We arrived at a park, and Manny helped me out of the car. He ran around to the back and pulled a basket out of the backseat. "I reserved the gazebo for us." Ahead of us was a charming shelter covered in white lights with a signed marked "Reserved."

Reaching for my hand, Manny tugged me forward. The rest of the park was practically deserted. The gazebo had a bench built around the interior part. He placed the basket on the bench, pulled a blanket from the top, and spread it on the floor in front of us.

"Ladies first." He motioned for me to sit and then followed suit behind me after he lowered the basket to the ground.

Inside was a vast arrangement of food. "It's not a fancy meal, but it's one of my favorites so I wanted to share it with you." Fried chicken tenders, sliced potatoes, and macaroni and cheese.

"It smells amazing."

"May I?" he asked, picking up a piece of chicken. I nodded. Holding the chicken out for me, I leaned forward, and he fed me a bite. Not sure if it was the company or if this was the best chicken I'd tasted in my life.

"Delicious." I grabbed a napkin to wipe away any trace of food on my face. "Why'd you pick this place?"

"It's not used much. A friend I work with had it built in memory of his wife who passed away." Just behind Manny, I spotted a plaque with a woman's name on it and a quote. "What a sweet tribute. Did you do anything like that for Connie?" He swallowed hard and looked away from me briefly.

"Sorry, that was too personal."

"Not at all. What is dating if not getting personal? You caught me off guard a little is all." Placing his food on the plate, he wiped his hands with a napkin and pulled out his phone.

"After Connie passed, I took her place on the road with Marie. At each stop along the way, we left a mark of Connie. In Seattle, I wrote Connie's name on the Volkswagen Beetle beneath the Freemont Troll."

"The one you see in *10 Things I Hate About You*?" He nodded.

"One of her favorite movies. She wanted to see it but never got to. Then when we were in Oregon, I carved our initials in a tree in the forest." He stopped talking.

"What else?"

"You don't want to hear about all of this. Ex-girlfriends on a date is a faux pas."

"She's not really an ex-girlfriend. She was so much more, wasn't she?" His gaze softened, a small smile appeared on his face.

"You're pretty amazing to understand, Perry." Rain began to drizzle down, each drop getting louder on the roof above us. "Looks like we might need to wait out the rain until my next part of the evening."

"Temperature dropped a bit," I commented, wrapping my arms around my middle.

"Stand up for a minute." I did as he asked, and he placed the food back in the basket, shook the blanket out, and wrapped it around my shoulders. "Now sit with me." Taking his seat on the floor with his back against the bench, I sat next to him and he placed his arm behind me. "Better?" Feeling his weight resting against mine calmed me, made me feel more comfortable with him. When I found comfort with someone in that way, I usually went from one extreme to another. From silent to rambling about every thought in my mind without considering the outcome.

"A little. Have you ever had weird thoughts go through your mind at random times?" His eyebrow cocked curiously at my question. "Like, who came up with rocky road ice cream?"

Manny chuckled. "Is that your favorite?" He grinned as I nodded enthusiastically. "Mine is just plain chocolate. I'm kind of boring in that way I guess."

"Nah, nothing boring about chocolate. What about

roller coasters? Who sat and thought, let's make this track out of wood and make people fly around it really fast until they want to throw up?" I sat forward, on a roll with my rambling ways. "And what about Jell-O? I mean that stuff is made from bone marrow of all things."

"Gross, I try not to think about how much of that I ate as a kid. Once I found out what it was made from, I never touched the stuff again. I think the last time I had it was when I was in the hospital having my tonsils removed. Do you have yours?"

I opened my mouth wide and said, "Ah."

Manny gawked. "Geez, woman, that tonsil is huge!"

"I know. I coughed so hard when I was younger that I coughed half of one up. The other one is always enlarged. I had strep so bad my throat almost closed off."

"Why'd you never have them removed?"

"Fear. The other side of anxiety is a fear of basically everything." Heights, bugs, death, ghosts, dolls, rejection, crowds, if there was something you could fear I most likely did.

"I'm afraid of clowns. Ever since I saw the movie *Poltergeist* and that clown doll under the bed came to life." I grinned at his admission and the look of horror on his face that was surprisingly adorable. "I had the same clown doll. We were watching it around Halloween that year, and as soon as I saw it in the movie, I grabbed the doll and threw it into the fire. My parents freaked out when I did it."

"I bet. I know exactly what doll you mean. I love horror movies, as long as they're slasher films. I can't stand ghosts or creepy kids, especially not ghost kids." I shivered as the thought of a ghostly child entered my mind. "I can read about them all day long, or write about them, but the visual will keep me up at night."

"*The Ring* kept me from sleeping with the TV on at night." Sliding around to face me, he continued. "I used to sleep with it on because I hated the silence in the room. Then one night I watched *The Ring* and woke up to the blue screen in the middle of the night and thought she was going to crawl out of the TV. I screamed and flipped the light on."

Living in the moment, I reached out to brush a stray hair from his face. He grinned at me. "Still attracted to me after hearing that story? I guess I could've made it worse if I'd wet the bed," he teased.

"I did that until I was in my teens. I was so embarrassed about it until I talked to a counselor who told me it's just something some kids go through and others don't. Lucky me to have such a trait. Does that make you feel better?" As I learned more about my anxiety, I believed bedwetting was one of the first symptoms.

Manny shook his head and showed me a sly grin. "You're adorable. If we're swapping embarrassing stories, I once leaned in to kiss a girl and I passed gas right when it happened. It was loud too."

Doubled over in laughter now, I pictured what Manny's face must have looked like when that happened. Between my fits of laughter, I heard him snort. "Did she die laughing?"

"No, she was disgusted and walked away. Wouldn't you have done the same thing?"

"No. Every human being on the planet farts. Unless you're like my cousin and born without an asshole." Both of us were in tears of laughter now.

"What?"

"No joke. He didn't live that way for long. It's called an imperforate anus and it takes a series of surgeries to create the normal opening. Once he had the surgeries to correct it, he was crawling along when he farted for the first time, and it scared the hell out of him." Neither of us could stop the laughing fits now. Manny had pulled me closer, and our bodies shook in unison.

We eventually stopped shaking, and the laughter subsided. We wiped away the tears that had fallen in the process.

"I haven't laughed that hard in a really long time." In fact, I couldn't remember the last time something made me truly laugh. Movies and TV shows made me laugh, but not a big belly laugh full of endorphins.

Manny was good for me, in so many ways.

Chapter Eleven

MANNY

Hearing Perry's laughter made my night complete. The twinkle in her eyes and the high-pitched sounds her laughter made, all of it was perfect. There were times in life I wished I could push pause, or rewind to relive them. I had several of those nights with Connie, and I counted this date as my first rewindable, pauseable moment with Perry.

"Wow, I didn't realize how late it had gotten." Beyond the gazebo was nothing but darkness. I peered down at my phone to check the time, and we'd been there for over three hours just laughing and talking.

"I like it here." Perry peered up at me with her big green eyes. She appeared so young and innocent in the moment.

"I like being here with you," I admitted. "Do you want to stay here for the evening or go to the next place I planned?"

"Depends. Is it half as awesome as this place? Because this was freaking amazing."

I glanced at my watch to check the time. "I think you'll

enjoy it. And we need to go soon if we're going to make it in time."

One of Dawn's customers ran a local business and offered to let me use it after closing this evening in exchange for working on her laptop when it crashed.

Perry didn't ask questions along the drive, seemingly content to be surprised this time. When I pulled into the parking lot, she turned to me. "Where are we?"

"Follow me and you'll see." Janice, Dawn's customer, had instructed me to knock on the receiving door in the back lot. I knocked three times and then stepped back so she could see me on the camera.

"Hey, Manny," Janice greeted as she opened the door. "You must be Perry?" Extending her hand to Perry, Janice offered a warm smile. "The place is all yours. Just lock up when you leave, and if you'll just hit the arm button on the alarm, it will set itself." She winked at Manny. "Enjoy."

"I'm confused," Perry said, looking ahead at the dark room. I stepped forward and turned on the light. Janice had shown me the track lighting and how to dim it enough that people didn't think the place was open.

"Is this the children's museum? I've never been here before." Like a kid on Christmas day, you could see the wonder in her eyes as she took in everything around her.

"As a boy, I came here all the time with my parents. It was my favorite place to go because I could face my fears and be anything I wanted to be." Perry appeared confused at how this was possible.

"For instance. Come in this room." I led her into the

next room and flipped on the switch. In front of us was a climbing wall that was only about ten feet tall since it was for children.

"Race you to the top?" At first, she acted confused and then shouted, "Ha," and ran forward, jumped up, grabbed hold of the rope, and began her climb. I ran up behind her, and we were both at the top of the wall in just a few steps.

At the peak, she threw her hands above her head and cheered. "What house are you?" she asked me suddenly.

"Hufflepuff," I answered, knowing exactly what she meant. I'd hopped on the Harry Potter bandwagon long ago; it was one of the few book series I'd read more than once. A true fan of the series knows which house they'd be sorted into.

"Me too!" She glanced across the room and shouted, "I want to fly the plane!" And I watched her jump back down to the ground and run over there before I followed her.

She took a seat in the front of the miniature airplane big enough for four to sit in. I made my way to the tower next to it and began messing with the radio. "Tower to gorgeous, this is Manny, come in, gorgeous."

"Gorgeous here, how's the weather down there, sexy?" Wow. I hadn't expected her to call me sexy. I liked it a lot. "Are we clear for landing?"

"You're clear as a bird. Come in slow and easy."

"Aww damn, and here I was hoping to come in fast and hard." Her words spoke straight to my cock. He sprang to life, and I suddenly felt very awkward having a raging hard-on while surrounded by toys. And Marie's comments about introverts being freaks in bed popped into my mind.

Perry jumped up and stepped out of the plane. "What's next?"

I grabbed her waist and pulled her toward me. Slowly I lowered my face to hers and before our lips met, I asked, "Is it clear for landing?"

"Free and clear, come in slow and easy." She repeated my words from a few moments before. Her lips grazed mine, and I felt her teeth tug at my lower lip gently. Pulling her closer I deepened the kiss. Our bodies were as close as they could get. The soft tug of her hands gripping my T-shirt, holding me to her, made me want more.

She jerked away from me and ran to another room. When I didn't follow right away, she ran back and motioned for me to follow her. "I thought you'd never been here before."

"I haven't, but I want to see it all."

The room she was in was one of my favorites as a kid. The Badger ship playroom. It was a model of the SS Badger, the ferryboat that traveled across Lake Michigan.

"Where did you go?"

"I'm up here," she shouted before she disappeared again. I heard a knocking coming from the slide on the left side of the ship, and I went to catch her at the bottom. She slid right into my arms, and I fell forward on top of her. Our lips crashed together once again.

I cut our kiss short this time and went on to the next section. When she came into the room, I had a postman's bag across my chest and I pulled out a letter. "Excuse me, are you—" I glanced down at the letter and pretended to read. "—award-winning author Perry Jordan?"

"Why, yes, I am, sir."

"I have your royalty check here. You're now officially richer than JK Rowling." Fist pumping the air, she cheered and jumped around.

"And you were just chosen to play the Dolby theater!"

"What?" Pointing to the sound stage setup, she grabbed the guitar and handed it to me.

"Dawn told me you like to play. So… play for me." I hadn't sung to anyone but Connie before. Dawn knew I could sing because she found a tape I made Connie once. When she was on the road, I wrote her a song and recorded it. Connie never had the chance to hear it though.

Pushing her bottom lip forward, she batted her eyes at me. "Please play?"

Strumming a few chords, I tried to figure out a song to sing. Once it came to me, I knew it was the perfect choice. I began to sing Blake Shelton's "A Guy with a Girl."

I put my own twist on it, with less twang and a little more of a soulful tone. My eyes were closed as I sang, but when I opened them, I saw tears in her eyes even though she had a smile on her face. I placed the guitar down and pulled her into my arms.

"This has been the best date, Manny. I'm not just saying that. It's like you took a chapter from my favorite romance novel and brought it to life." I brushed a hair out of her eyes and kissed her nose.

"I was going for as romantic as possible."

"You succeeded. I've had the best time tonight." She wrapped her arms around my neck in a tight hug. I relished the moment holding her close, inhaling the sweet strawberry scent wafting from her hair. "You always smell like strawberries," I mumbled.

I felt her breath against my ear as she whispered, "I don't want this night to end."

The truth was, I didn't want it to either. "We have several more hours. We can watch the sun come up together if you want."

"I know I don't want to go home yet."

"Then we won't." She followed me to the next room. The setup contained a make-believe ice cream parlor. I packed a cone with six scoops and handed it to Perry.

She covered her mouth and shook her head. In a high-pitched southern drawl, she commented, "It'll go straight to my hips."

"I like curvy girls," I said with a twang in my own attempt at an accent. "Seriously. I think women of all shapes, sizes, and colors are beautiful as long as they're beautiful on the inside too." I cringed at my own words. "Sounded cheesier than I intended."

"No, it didn't. It sounded wonderful. The world needs more Mannys in it." Perry crossed the room and sat down on the couch. She patted the seat next to her. Again, I followed her command.

She placed her head against my shoulder, and I laid mine on hers. "Have you had some rotten dates?"

"Nothing particularly horrible. And I'm still single so I

haven't had any particularly amazing ones either." Shifting her weight, she moved her head. Immediately I missed the contact.

"Was there ever anyone other than Connie who you were in love with?"

"No." Apparently, she expected a longer answer because she stared at me with wondering eyes. "Before Connie, I was a ladies' man. To be honest, when Brady asked me to go on the trip with him and told me about Marie's friend, I assumed we'd probably hook up once or twice and that would be it."

"Did you ever tell her?"

"Yep. She said she felt the same way. She told me it was what she hoped for. A little fling on the road to sow her wild oats. Neither of us expected to fall in love so quickly."

Perry fidgeted with a string on her pants. Eye contact with me had been dropped. "I don't mean to talk about her so much, but you keep asking."

"I know. I like hearing about her. Sounds like you two had the kind of love I write about in my books. Gives me inspiration in a way."

I yawned and stretched my arms above my head. "It's late. I think I should probably drive you home."

Judging by the look on her face, I knew she was confused by my sudden interest in leaving. Talking about Connie was still hard for me. I wanted to move forward. If I wanted to do that with Perry, and I did, then I needed to push Connie to the back of my thoughts and my heart.

Perry followed me to the back door. She stepped outside

while I turned off the lights, pushed the button on the alarm and closed the door behind me.

I reached for her hand and led her to the passenger's side door of my car. "I had a lot of fun tonight, Perry. I hope you did."

"I did. Best second date ever."

"Or was it the second-best date ever?" I teased. Her sad smile damaged my pride. Just an hour ago, she had been laughing and now she seemed so sad. "I had a great night, Perry. It's hard to talk about Connie though."

"I'm sorry for bringing her up. I was curious."

"I understand." Conversation on the ride home was scarce. I loved how much she'd opened up to me, but like a switch had been flipped, she went back to the quiet, fidgety woman from our first date. When I dropped Perry off at her apartment, she gave me a quick kiss goodnight at the door, followed by a smile, and said, "See you around. Thanks again for tonight."

The words sounded promising, but her tone left me feeling as though there may not be a third date.

Chapter Twelve

The night with Manny was perfect, until it ended. I knew I'd screwed up by bringing up Connie, but I also knew he didn't hate me for it. I wouldn't let my anxiety or insecurities ruin this for me.

Though I'd been quiet on the ride home, I'd wanted to invite him in but had lost my confidence. After he left, looking a little downtrodden, I took the initiative and sent him a text.

Me: Tonight was perfect.

Manny: Which part?

Me: All of it. Thank you.

Manny: My pleasure, sweetheart.

Me: Guess you need to start planning date three to outdo tonight.

Manny: I'm already working on it. ;)

Me: Good night.

Manny: Sweet dreams.

Sending the text was the perfect idea. As soon as my head hit the pillow, I fell straight to sleep. For the first time in a long time, I slept through the night.

* * *

The next morning, I received an email from my publisher asking me to sign up for another book event. "You're killing me, Smalls," I mumbled to the empty room, quoting the movie *The Sandlot*, a favorite from my childhood.

The email contained a form to fill in, so I reluctantly put in all my information and asked for a payment plan. I had another two months before the event in Frankenmuth and almost six before this one.

Pushing them out was great for giving me time to prepare for the overwhelming panic attacks.

Manny: Did you sleep well?

Me: I did. Best night's sleep in a while.

Manny: Want to meet for lunch tomorrow?

Me: Date three already?

Manny: Why wait? They say third time is the charm.

Me: I'm not sure you can top the first two.

Manny: Challenge accepted.

Me: lol. Noon tomorrow?

Manny: I'll pick you up. See you then.

A thought occurred to me and I decided to google "How many dates before it's a relationship?" And the result was a paragraph telling me that every relationship was different and there was no set amount of dates.

"Google, you've failed this introvert," I mumbled. Another search that caught my eye read "What is the three-date rule?"

According to the powers that be of the internet, the third date was the appropriate time to have sex with a guy. "So, Google can't tell me how many dates are considered a relationship, but it knew three dates was the magic number for sex." I had a habit of talking to myself out loud when I was home alone.

After searching for answers, I felt more clueless than ever. I knew the internet wasn't the best source of information, but I didn't have many options.

Glancing down at the phone, I decided to connect with a human being instead of a machine.

Me: How many dates did you and Brady go on before you called yourself a couple?

Dawn: I don't remember counting.

Me: I'm overthinking things, aren't I?

Dawn: No, it's a valid question.

Dawn: We knew each other for six months before we moved in together, does that help?

Me: Opened up a little extra anxiety actually.

Dawn: lol, Sorry.

Another failure at finding the answers I needed led me to one more option. "Magic Eight ball, is three the magic number for dating?" I shook up the ball and sighed. Reply: "hazy, try again." That's the way my life always goes.

One of the most popular questions I saw on Facebook

was regarding what superpower you'd want. Having psychic abilities, the power to see the future, would either be the best thing for my anxiety or the worst.

For instance, the best thing would be not going through every possible scenario and assuming the worst would happen. On the other hand, knowing what was about to occur could also send me into a tailspin panic.

I closed the laptop. "Get a grip, Perry. You just had two of the best dates of your entire life with a guy who treated you like a princess even after you showed him your crazy." Putting positivity down on paper, or in text form at least, helped me to stick to it.

Me: It's fine. I'm going to choose to remain positive. Manny seems like a great guy, and I want to give this a chance to turn into something great.

Dawn: Great attitude to have! I promise, he's worth taking a chance on.

Even in the short time I'd known him, I knew Dawn was right. Manny was worth it.

Chapter Thirteen

MANNY

Date two started off fantastic and ended as a bit of a drag. I needed to be sure date three went perfectly. My first mistake was promising Perry I'd make it even better than date two. I used all my best ideas on that date.

Thankfully I had my job to occupy my mind for the moment. Working at home, making my own hours, had its perks. While busy on my laptop, waiting for my files to load, I started googling ideas.

The file finished downloading before I could come up with anything. Diving headfirst into work, I began trying out the newest video game my company was interested in purchasing the rights to. A game for adults that made *Grand Theft Auto* look somewhat tame in comparison. The description of the game had promised it would put *GTA* to shame, but instead I was ashamed to play it.

Basically, the game was about a necrophiliac serial killer. Some sick fuck came up with the idea it would be fun to run around town killing people and screwing them. After forcing myself to go through three levels, I turned it off and wrote a review to send to my boss with the highlights of the horrifying game. A few minutes after I sent it, he told me to scrap the file and he'd give them a proper letdown.

As I grabbed file two, I had an idea. I shot a text to Perry.

Me: Do you like video games?

Perry: Depends on the type of game. I'm not great at most of them.

Me: Doesn't matter. It's all for fun. Would you like to come to my place and help me test some?

Perry: Sure. When?

Me: Now? You could bring lunch, and I'll pay you when you get here?

Perry: Pizza?

Me: Sounds great. Actually I'll order it. Just head over.

Perry: Send me your address.

Once I sent it to her, I ran around the room straightening things as quickly as I could. Then I dialed up my favorite pizza place, put in an order, and hung up in time for Perry to knock on the door.

"I brought movies in case I royally suck at the video games, as usual." In her hands, she had three movies. Even if they ended up being all mushy chick flicks, I loved that she brought several hours of entertainment for us. She wanted to stick around for a while.

"I think you'll like this game. I have to test them for work, and the last one I tried was terrible. I'll spare you."

"How bad could it have been?" she asked.

"One word… necrophilia."

"Wow. That's enough detail for me to stay away." She set her movies down on the table and plopped her bottom on the couch. Respecting her boundaries, I sat on the opposite end, leaving enough room between us for another person.

My body was drawn to her. Like a magnet trying to connect with another one nearby, every inch of me strained to be closer to her. Based on her body language, she felt something at least similar. She adjusted in her seat several times, crossing one leg over the other and moving her hands from atop her knees to underneath her thighs.

Grabbing two controllers from the coffee table, I handed one to Perry. "I'll let you go first."

"Great. I told you I suck at these."

"Trust me, you'll be fine." I grinned mischievously as I turned the game on. She stared at the screen a moment and then doubled over in laughter. I'd chosen a preschool age game from the pile. One with cartoon penguins. To move them along the board the player had to correct grammar mishaps.

Perry read from the screen, "Peggy the Penguin loves to visit her siblings. Together they love to practice perfect grammar. Find the mistakes in the text so they can move along to the next room." Clicking to go to the next screen, she read the first line, "*Their* going to the fair." She cringed as she started correcting the issue. "I despise the misuse of their, there, and they're when I see it. If people just stop to consider what they're writing, they wouldn't screw it up."

Perry soared through six of the seven levels in a matter of minutes. The game was incredibly easy for someone used to grammar. For me, it took three times as long to get to the levels she reached. "Do you like kids?" I asked her.

"Of course. Why do you ask?"

"Would you mind if I invited a neighbor over to help with this game. He's seven, and I need to see how easy this is for the correct age range. If it makes you uncomfortable—"

"Not at all," Perry stated, interrupting me. "People make me nervous because I never know what they're thinking. Kids are honest to a fault most of the time. It's refreshing."

"I'll be right back." Sprinting down the stairs and across the courtyard, I knocked on my neighbor Annie's door.

"Manny!" Annie exclaimed. As a single mom, she'd told me never to hesitate to stop by and visit because she always yearned for more adult interaction. As attractive as she was, we never hit it off romantically, but we worked well as friends though. "Come in, please!" By the urgency in her tone, I knew the little guy was driving her batty.

"I wondered if I could take Jude off your hands for a bit. I need help with one of my games."

Her expression went from one of exhaustion to real excitement. "Can he stay with you for two to three hours?" Glancing back over her shoulder and then leaning forward, she whispered, "His birthday is coming up, and I never get a chance to shop without him."

"Um…" I looked back toward my apartment, hoping Perry meant it when she said she liked kids. When I turned back to see the look of pleading in Annie's eyes, I had no choice. "Sure, no problem. My friend Perry is over helping me with the game as well. We ordered pizza that will be here any minute. She's waiting on the delivery guy. Has he eaten?"

With a knowing grin, she grabbed my hand. "You know you have to tell me about her later. No. We haven't eaten, and pizza is his favorite." Leaving me standing at the door, she came back a moment later with Jude next to her.

"Hey, buddy," I said as Jude peered up at me with his big brown eyes. "Want to come hang out and play video games?"

Looking to his mom for permission, she nodded in agreement. "Yes!" Jude jumped up and down clapping his hands. He tried to run out the door right away, but Annie reached out to stop him. "Take your backpack please." Handing it to Jude, she addressed me. "Inside, he has a few snacks and his inhaler in case he has any trouble breathing." Kneeling down to Jude's level, she caressed his cheek with her thumb. "You be good for Manny and his friend Perry please." Occasionally I take Jude off Annie's hands to give her a break. Never once had he acted anything but spectacular. She'd raised the kid to be the perfect gentleman. His father was a deadbeat who dropped her the minute she told him she was pregnant, but she told Jude stories of his dad. They were true stories, of his time in the military and things he did for others, she just left out the part where he never wanted to be a dad.

Jude held out his hand to me. Annie had a rule he always had to hold my hand when we weren't in the house. "Who's Perry, Uncle Manny?" I wasn't related to him in the least, but I loved him calling me uncle. I didn't have any biological nieces or nephews, so it made me feel important.

"Perry is a friend of mine." When we reached the door, I leaned down to him. "Perry can be a little shy, so you might have to help me get her to talk."

"I can make anybody talk," he stated proudly. Perry was on the couch where I left her. Jude's eyes grew wide when he saw the TV screen. "Penguins!"

"Penguins are my favorite. I think they're so funny," Perry stated.

"She talks just fine, Uncle Manny." Perry sucked her lips between her teeth to keep from laughing. My face heated, probably turning at least two to three shades of pink.

"The pizza arrived while you were gone. I hope Jude is hungry."

With a loud, dramatic sniff, Jude breathed in. "Pizza's my favorite!"

Perry was great with Jude. Neither of them seemed to notice I was there for a bit as they bonded over their love of penguins. After eating, they played a few rounds of the game. Confidence in my intelligence waned as I watched Jude fly through the levels almost as easily as Perry had done.

"Manny isn't really my uncle. He's a friend of my mom's. He comes around a lot because I don't have a dad. Mom told me to call him uncle because he's like the brother she always wanted." Jude rattled on, and Perry listened intently. "I didn't always understand what that meant until I got older and figured out he's the dad I always wanted."

"I know exactly what you mean," Perry replied.

"You want Manny to be your dad too?" he asked, his face scrunched up in confusion as his eyes were pointed toward the ceiling in thought.

Perry laughed. "No. I just meant I can understand what you're trying to say. Manny is pretty awesome." A man's ego could burst listening to the two of them carrying on.

"I think you're both pretty awesome too."

Jude and Perry grinned up at me. "Come join us in the game," Jude asked.

"It's only a two-player. I like watching though."

While they played some more, I started wrapping the leftovers. Cold pizza would be a perfect breakfast tomorrow. I was in the kitchen for a bit cleaning up and putting away dishes. I stuck my head back in the room to check on things. Before I said anything, I listened to their conversation.

"Did Manny tell you I have trouble breathing?" Jude asked her. Being born with a bronchial defect was why he kept an inhaler on him. "He saved my life once." A slight exaggeration but mostly true. The first time I met Annie she was calling out for Jude. He'd been playing outside while she was cooking dinner. She was yelling for him to come inside. I'd been working on my truck at the time and heard her voice become more panicked the more she said his name.

I introduced myself to her, asked if I could help, and we began the search. We went different ways around the building, and when I found Jude he was under a tree on his back. His face had turned blue. I gave him CPR until he started coughing. Annie came around the corner frantic.

"He has asthma! Is he okay?"

Jude sat up with my help. "I'm Manny, buddy. You feeling okay now?" He nodded, and Annie threw her arms around him as soon as she knew it was safe.

Perry lowered her voice. "He kind of saved my life too. He doesn't know it yet though." I ducked back out of sight before she knew I'd heard. I wasn't sure what she meant or if I should even ask her later.

"When we did a paper at school recently about our favorite superhero, I wrote about Manny." Once again, my curiosity was piqued so I peered around the corner in time to see Jude grab his backpack. "I have it in here. Do you want to read it?"

"Sure," Perry said. Unfolding the piece of paper, she began to read it out loud. "My Uncle Manny is my favorite superhero. He may not have an iron suit or be able to climb walls like a spider, but he gave me air. Air helps us live. Superheroes save lives, and my Uncle Manny saved mine."

The kid was good for a man's ego, that I could testify to for sure.

"You should show this to Manny."

"Mom said I could give it to him. I thought he might want to hang it on his fridge like my mom hangs up stuff I draw for her. Do you think he'll like it or think it's dumb?"

Perry handed him the paper. "I think it will make him smile. Why don't you run in there to hand it to him now?" Without making a sound, I inched back into the kitchen to make myself look busy.

Jude came through the doorway looking a bit

apprehensive. "What's up, buddy?" He chewed on his bottom lip as he looked back and forth between the paper in his hand and me.

"What's that?" I pretended to be oblivious. Timidly he held his hand out to me with the paper. "For me?" He nodded. I opened it up, read the same words Perry had read a moment ago. After finishing it, I grinned as widely as I could and said, "Jude, this is the coolest thing anyone has ever done for me. I wish I had a copy I could put on my fridge."

Jude beamed with pride. "You can hang that one on your fridge." He watched while I grabbed a magnet and placed it directly under a picture of Constance.

"Is Perry your girlfriend?" he asked out of the blue. When I didn't answer, he continued. "I like her."

"You know what? I like her too," I said. Standing in the doorway, I looked up in time to see Perry with a pleased look on her face. I think I succeeded in my challenge for making the third date great.

Chapter Fourteen

PERRY

August had arrived, but I wasn't confident enough with Manny to ask him to attend the conference with me. We'd been dating for a few months now. I'd lost track of what number date it was. Mostly I kept track of the months instead of the number of dates. Each date he did something to make it special.

As the book signing came closer, he'd hinted around about going with me, but I never had the courage to call him out on it. Every time he brought it up, I wanted to tell him to please come. The morning I left, he wished me luck by text during my drive.

Three nerve-filled hours later, after two U-turns and trying to talk myself out of bailing, I arrived. The inn where the signing took place was massive. I could get lost inside, and the thought gave me peace instead of more nerves. My superhero power was invisibility. I knew how to blend.

The thought made me smile as I remembered Jude's

report about Manny. Since our third date, we'd had Jude over a few times. Manny had introduced me to Annie, his mom, so she would be comfortable with me hanging around. I'd grown to love the kid almost as though he were my own. One day he heard me mention my writing. His eyes were so wide with awe as I showed him my books were available online. The next week at school, he asked to take one of my books for show and tell. Of course I sent one of my YA novels and not any of the adult romances. I promised him I'd have someone take a picture of me signing books over the weekend. Maybe I'd get my tablemate to agree to it for me.

The signing event lasted from midday Friday through all of Saturday. On Friday morning, I had to check in to the hotel first, and then I spent the next few hours in my room freaking out about attending the ball. Knowing masks were involved was the thing keeping me going.

Me: I arrived at the hotel.

Manny: Stay calm, you're going to be amazing tomorrow. Just relax, sweetheart.

When he called me sweetheart, it made my toes curl and I couldn't wipe the smile off my face if I tried. Once I was in the comfort of my room, I put my luggage in the corner, slipped off my shoes, and stepped out onto the balcony. There was a small table outside, so I brought along my mini–word processor and began to work on my next book. Once the light started to fade making it hard to read the screen, I headed inside to get ready for the dinner and ball.

More than ever, I wished I'd invited Manny, or even

Dawn, someone to use as a crutch to hide my awkwardness a little. Though I knew it was a costume ball and had seen several people share their outfits, I still had the irrational fear that I'd be the only one in costume and everyone would laugh at me. The "Carrie at the prom" nightmare was one I had on a regular basis.

Just as I was about to get ready, my phone rang. I hoped it was Manny, but it was my dad instead. My parents were two of the few people I knew who owned a landline, so when they called from the house, I wasn't sure who I'd hear on the other end of the line. On a normal day, I dreaded phone calls. Answering the call at that moment meant I would delay heading to the party. Any delay from social interaction was welcomed.

"Hello?"

"Hey, honey. I haven't heard your voice in a while and wanted to check in." My dad's voice came through the line instantly putting a grin on my face. No matter how much of a loner I was, I was also a daddy's girl.

"Hey, Dad. I'm sorry, things have been hectic lately with writing and… stuff."

"And stuff? What kind of stuff?" News of my relationship, or whatever, with Manny had not been passed around to my parents yet. I wasn't ready for all the questions.

"I'm in Frankenmuth for a book signing this weekend. You know it's not really my thing to do events like this. I've been a bit stressed." The stress didn't keep me busy with Manny in my life, but I still didn't lie to my dad.

"Did a friend go with you?"

"No, I came alone." Not by choice was what I wanted to add.

"I don't like you driving alone, honey," he chided.

"I'm fine, Daddy. I promise." I glanced at the clock. "I need to go. I'll call you when I get home in a few days."

"Be safe, Peregrin." I made a promise to him I would be and that I'd text or call each day to let him know how things were. He was a worrier, which was genetic apparently. All I did was worry… about every little thing.

I put on my blue goddess gown and slipped a mask, adorned with gold, over my face. The mask wasn't necessary for my costume, but it *was* for my sanity. With the immensity of the hotel, I took full advantage of getting lost on my way to the ball. When I saw the sign letting me know I was in the correct place, my body tensed with nerves. A panic attack loomed nearby.

Given the choice of stairs or elevator, I chose the elevator. Even though it was only one flight of stairs to the ballroom, my body shook so much I was terrified of tripping and injuring myself. The humiliation would be more painful than any broken teeth or bruises, but I didn't want to risk any of it. For just one floor, the elevator was the slowest I'd ever been on. For a moment I didn't think it was moving and a heavy weight fell on my chest. *How will I get out if it's stuck? Will I have the courage to call for help? How long will I be stuck in here?* The air in the small space grew denser. As soon as the bell sounded, I sucked in a long breath. The doors opened, and I stumbled forward anxious to be in a larger space.

From the elevator, I had to walk around the open area where the stairs were to get to the ballroom. Between my destination and me stood at least thirty people I would pass by. Suddenly I wished I'd gotten stuck on the elevator instead. As quickly as possible, I shuffled past the groups of people chatting. The man at the door waved me through, obviously spotting the author badge in the lanyard around my neck.

Finding a table all the way in the back with very few people, I sat at the end away from anyone and kept to myself. The food was set up buffet style, which saved me the struggle of deciding on a meal. Every decision seemed life changing, as though picking the wrong thing would send me down some crazy path. My stomach growled as the scent of fried chicken wafted through the air. The town was apparently famous for their chicken. I stacked my plate with a little of everything.

During dinner, the people at the table chatted, and occasionally they'd ask me questions. Curt answers popped from my lips. I wanted to be sociable, but I couldn't find the strength. An ironic fact about me, I found strength in numbers but couldn't find the strength to obtain the numbers. In other words, when accompanied by friends, I could open up, but finding friends was even harder than trying to open up on my own. Eventually they stopped trying to include me.

The struggle to socialize was exhausting, and the aftermath brought depression. I kept imagining a moment where Manny walked inside and swept me off my feet, saving me from myself, but it didn't happen. The large room began to close in around me. My skin dampened with sweat and my breath quickened. I slipped out after making myself sit there for an hour without speaking to anyone.

Back in my hotel room, I was exhausted from the sheer effort of being in a crowd trying to remain calm. Since the signing began early the next day, I called it a night. Just before turning in, I sent a text to Manny.

Me: The ball didn't go so well. Hopefully tomorrow will be better.

Manny: It will. Text me if you need me.

Me: Thanks, handsome.

Manny: Ooh, I like when you call me handsome. *wink*

Having been together for a while now made me more comfortable being flirty. We hadn't pronounced any feelings or taken the next step, just had a lot of great make-out sessions so far. Come to think of it, we hadn't labeled ourselves as boyfriend and girlfriend either.

In my books, my hero and heroine always had cutesy little names for each other, and I wanted to try one with Manny but hadn't found anything I liked yet. Handsome suited him well though.

I added a few lines of sweetness.

Me: I wish you were here. I sort of miss you.

Manny: Only sort of?

Me: Don't push it.

Manny: Lol. I miss you too, sweetheart.

Me: I like when you call me sweetheart. I better get

some rest.

Manny: Goodnight, sweetheart. Sweet dreams.

Me: Same to you.

Me: Handsome.

Instead of responding with words, he sent me a selfie of him smiling. I kissed the phone wishing it were him instead. Who knew I'd become the woman crazy enough to be so mushy over a man.

Chapter Fifteen

MANNY

When Perry told me about her signing in Frankenmuth, I hadn't wanted to intrude. I'd considered inviting myself along or just showing up, but I didn't want to spook her. When she said she missed me and wished I was there, I made up my mind.

The signing began at ten and I had a three-hour drive ahead of me. I left my house around seven to get there in plenty of time without spooking her before it began.

With the number of signs posted for the event I found it rather quickly. At the front door, I asked to be pointed in the direction of the correct author. The young lady checked her chart and sent me on my way inside. With what looked to be a hundred author names on the sheet, I was glad I asked.

Once inside, I was amazed and proud to know Perry agreed to such a massive event. Her table was in the corner toward the back. As I watched her, I noticed she kept her head down, focused on writing on her little contraption.

Her face was drained of all color. As she tried to type, her hands trembled. Desperately trying to hold onto her sanity, she was on the brink of an anxiety attack. I hoped coming wouldn't make it worse. I approached her cautiously and said, "Hello, sweetheart," when I reached her table.

She peered up at me confused for a moment, shook her head, and went back to writing. "Perry?" I said again, wondering what just happened. Again, she glanced up, looked around, and shook her head.

"Sir?" the author next to her said. "Would you like to see my books?"

Perry looked to her neighbor, then back up at me, and the confusion left her face and was replaced with elation. "You're here!" She jumped up, raced around the table, and threw her arms around my neck, almost knocking me backward.

"Now that's a better reaction!" I hugged her close to me inhaling the sweet scent I loved so much. *Strawberries*.

She whispered in my ear, "I thought I was imagining you like last night. I'm so glad you're here." Neither reaction had been what I expected to receive, but I loved the second one. I'd never seen her look so happy or so relieved.

"Let me grab you a chair." She started to leave and turned back. "You're staying, right?"

"Absolutely, sweetheart. But you sit down and let me get the chair." When I came back, I placed the chair next to her and she reached for my hand. Being affectionate hadn't been her thing before, but as I held her hand, I felt her body calming.

I kissed the back of her hand and passed along a red rose to her. "Congratulations on your first signing. I want to take you out for dinner afterward if you'd like."

"That would be great."

From that moment forward, I noticed people would stop at her table and speak to her. I assumed it was due to the fact she had a smile on her face and appeared approachable instead of drowning in her own little world. My chest swelled with pride as each person stopped to check out her books. When she would stumble over her words, I'd place my hand on her shoulder and help her by saying something funny or talking about the ones I'd read. She had six books out, and I'd read three of them now. Romance books weren't my thing usually, but I enjoyed hers. The amount of pop culture references she wrote about made it easier to relate.

After a while, I noticed Perry's ability to talk to people became much less of a strain on her. I'd helped her track the number of sales she had once I arrived. At the end of the day I saw a full page of inventory listed as sold. When I looked over to see how she was doing, she had a glow about her. Hearing people gush over my girlfriend, seeing them light up over her books and put a smile on her face, made my day. The whole event was surreal. I couldn't imagine how it felt for Perry.

As the crowd began to die down, she settled into her seat and relaxed. "I wish I'd booked my room for a second night. I forgot how exhausting all this talking can be for me," she stated, leaning her head against my shoulder. I loved when she snuggled on me; it felt nice to be needed.

"I booked a room at the hotel down the street because I wasn't sure if you were going to be here tonight or not. You're welcome to stay with me. Or take it for yourself if you'd prefer."

She peered up at me, her tired eyes suddenly sparkled with life. "I'll stay with you, if you don't mind."

"Of course I don't. I'd love it." Leaning forward, I kissed her lips quickly. I knew she wasn't much of a PDA kind of woman. "And I'll call and see if I can get the room switched to a double."

"No need. We can share, if you—"

Before she could ask if I minded again, I interrupted her words with another kiss. "I have no qualms about cuddling with you tonight."

Pressing her mouth against my ear, she whispered, "We may do more than cuddle if you're up for it." I was up for it, literally. My dick sprang to life the moment her lips grazed my ear. Taking things slowly had been the best for both of us. We hadn't spent the night together yet; this would be a first we could cross off our imaginary list of relationship steps.

When we got to the room later that evening, we both wanted to shower before heading out to grab dinner. Perry went first, and then when I got out, she was on the bed wearing only my T-shirt and probably panties, though I couldn't tell. She had lain down and curled into a fetal position and fallen asleep. Wearing nothing but boxer briefs, I slid into the bed beside her and set an alarm on my phone for a couple of hours. I started to drift off when I felt her roll over, toss her leg across my body, and her arm across my chest.

I snuggled closer to her, enjoying the warmth of her body and having contact with her in general. The closer we became, the more comfortable she grew with me. She would hug me now without thinking twice about it, and sometimes in public, she'd take my hand as we walked. I always let her make the first move because I knew her boundaries were different than mine, and I respected them as much as possible.

Our relationship was different than mine with Connie. Connie and I were together a short time, and everything moved at warp speed. The slow pace with Perry was a nice change.

I listened to her snore lightly, almost like a purring kitten. Just before nodding off, I kissed her forehead gently and placed my arm against her back.

When I awoke, Perry was still sleeping in my arms and it was two hours later. She'd told me how worn out she gets in social situations, but I had no idea how accurate she was. I thought it might have been an exaggeration. I stood corrected.

"Perry?" I whispered lightly against her ear. She didn't move, but her chest rose and fell slowly. I slid out from under her and just as I got up off the bed, I heard, "What time is it?" in her soft, and a little scratchy, just-woke-up voice.

She stretched and yawned. "It's around eight," I told her. Her eyes widened. "It's fine, you must have been worn out."

"I was. Are you still hungry or did you go eat?"

"I lay down with you and was just getting up to stretch and woke you up."

"I'm glad you did. Give me a few minutes to get dressed and we can grab dinner." Her stomach growled loudly at that exact moment. "Apparently I'm starving," she said with a giggle.

Ten minutes later, we were walking down the street toward a small eatery I'd seen on the way into town. I'd looked the menu up online to see what they had while Perry was getting dressed. My mouth started watering when I saw the mac-in-awe pizza, macaroni and cheese pizza with ham cubes.

Perry reached for my hand about a block from the hotel. Trying not to embarrass her, I simply smiled to avoid making a big deal over the gesture. We sat down, ordered dinner and an appetizer of fried peanut butter and jelly sticks. The pizza came out looking better than what I had imagined, and we both grabbed a few pieces off the tray and placed them on our plates.

"I can't tell you how much it means to me that you came here, Manny. I had dreaded this event from the moment I scheduled it. Not the event itself, just the size of the crowds and the sheer terror of having to speak to people." She paused and placed her hand over mine. "Having you here made it a lot easier on me. A friendly face was exactly what I needed."

"I was afraid you'd be mad I showed up. I'm glad to have been wrong."

"I wanted to ask you to come. I was afraid you'd think it

was weird or too soon." She blushed and lowered her gaze to the table. "The reason I didn't answer you when you first came to the table was because at the ball, I spent the entire time imagining you showing up, and I thought my mind was playing tricks on me again."

Damn. I wished I had played the gallant knight by showing up for her at the ball instead. That would have been epic romance material, but it's too late for should've been.

"I wish I'd known. It wasn't until last night when you said you wished I was here that I thought about taking the chance of surprising you." Rephrasing slightly, I said, "I mean, I thought about it before that, but once you said it, I knew it was a good idea. Or hoped it was at least. Does anything I said make sense?"

Perry laughed and covered her mouth to hide the bite of food she'd taken. "You've become a rambler like me."

"Guess you're rubbing off on me. After dinner where do you want to go?"

"We could just walk the street a little." I paid the tab and we headed out. Most of the small shops were getting ready to close, but the temperature wasn't too bad for just a stroll. I spotted a horse-drawn carriage and took a shot. "Can I treat you to a carriage ride?"

"I've always wanted to do that," she exclaimed with genuine excitement. Though the price was a little steep for the short ride, it was worth it to fulfill something she'd wanted to do. I lifted her up into the carriage and then followed her. I raised my arm and placed it behind her on the bench, and she leaned in close to me, so I draped it over her shoulder for the ride.

"How often do they do this book event?" I asked.

"Annually. Authors attending get first dibs on tables next year, but I'm not sure if I can handle it again."

"What if I come with you for the long-haul next time? We could invite Brady and Dawn along and have a couples' weekend."

Moving away from me just enough to meet my eyes, hers widened with question. "That's a year away. Are you sure you can put up with me for that long?"

I chuckled before realizing she was serious. "Perry, if things keep going as well as they have with us, I can see a few years ahead with you. I enjoy our time together."

She pulled away, and I feared I'd said too much. And then she asked, "How much time do you get off work?"

"A lot. I pretty much make my own hours, why?"

"When you traveled with Marie, did it affect your job?"

"Not really. What's on your mind, Perry?"

"My publisher wants me to do more signings and most require traveling. They're spread out around the country, but I know of a few big ones like in St. Louis, Nashville, and I think there's even one in Chattanooga if you wanted to go and visit Marie." All of this flew out of her mouth in record speed as though she was trying to get it out in one breath.

"I think that would be a lot of fun. When we get to the hotel, why don't we look some up on your laptop and see if we can come up with a schedule."

The thing I loved most... wait... liked? I'm not sure

whether I loved Perry yet or not, but I knew one thing, putting a smile on her face was my mission every time we were together, and today the mission had been accomplished more than once.

For the rest of the ride, Perry stayed curled up next to me, and when the carriage reached our hotel, she was asleep on my shoulder. "Can you let us out here?" I whispered to the coach.

"Sure. Have a good evening, sir."

Moving my arm from behind her, I stepped down from the coach before attempting to wake her. She stood, still half asleep, and I lifted her off the platform and down onto the concrete. She struggled to get inside, yawning repeatedly. Once we got off the elevator on our floor, I lifted her up. She squeaked with surprise, and I carried her down the hall. Though it was a short walk to our room, she fell asleep with her head on my shoulder.

Placing her down on the bed I took off her shoes, unhooked her bra, and removed it without removing her shirt so I protected her modesty, and then covered her with the blanket.

My phone dinged. I quickly silenced it so she could sleep.

Dawn: How did the surprise go?

Me: Perfectly. Made her smile.

Dawn: Did you stay the night?"

Me: Yep. She's sleeping now. She had no room tonight but wanted to stay with me.

Dawn: Progress!

Me: That was my thought. She's opening up a lot more. I'll talk to you when I get back. I'm hitting the sack.

Dawn: Good night. Be safe coming home tomorrow!
Me: Will do.

I crawled into bed next to Perry and watched her sleep for just a few moments as I drifted off into my own slumber. In the middle of the night, I was awoken with a strong kick to my shin, and I bolted up in the bed and grabbed my leg.

Perry thrashed around the bed, whimpering in her sleep. I placed my hand on her shoulder, and she mumbled, "Manny?"

"It's me, sweetheart. Are you all right?"

"Mmmhmm" was all she said before she began to snore all over again. Most of the time, I didn't sleep over at a woman's house, so the only person I'd been used to was Connie, and she slept like a peaceful angel. Getting used to Perry's thrashing and obvious nightmares would take time. I hoped to get the time to adjust though. Minus the throbbing pain in my shin and the rude awakening, I enjoyed being next to her.

Chapter Sixteen

PERRY

Throughout the night I had one bad dream after the next. There were few details I remembered, but they all revolved around Manny telling me I was crazy and leaving me for another woman. The woman was petite with an auburn pixie-cut hairstyle. I wondered if my subconscious was worried about his lost love. I'd never seen a photo, but Marie and Dawn had described her to me.

My dream didn't depict her the way they described though, not personality wise at least. She kept telling me I wasn't good enough for Manny and how I needed to stop wasting his time.

The carriage ride we shared had meant a lot to me. Ever since I was a little girl, I dreamed of those romantic gestures from a man, but I'd never found one who took the time to make any of them come true until Manny. Historically, my dates before Manny had been boring. Dinner, with awkward, limited conversation, and a movie where I didn't have to talk, but the man just wanted to grope me instead of watching the film. Manny put thought into every date.

I was falling for him. I knew it to be true, even if I wasn't sure what being in love felt like. He was quickly taking over my heart, and if I wasn't careful, he'd shatter me into a million pieces with a snap of his fingers.

When morning came, he was still asleep, and I admit being kind of stalkery as I watched him. He smiled in his peaceful state. I hoped that meant he was having a happy dream. I yawned and caught a whiff of my breath in the air. I crept out of the bed and snuck into the bathroom to brush my teeth before he woke.

"Perry?" I heard from the other room.

"Be right out," I said, foaming at the mouth with toothpaste. Cupping my hand under the faucet, I filled it with water and tossed it back into my mouth, swished the contents, and spat just in time to look up and see Manny standing outside the door I'd left open in my haste.

"Well that was a sexy thing to witness, I'm sure," I joked as I wiped the moisture off my mouth.

"Everything about you is pretty sexy so far." He complimented me, again. I never knew how to respond to his sweet words other than giggling and lowering my head to hide my reddening face.

Leaning in, he stopped just short of my lips as though asking permission to kiss me. I closed the gap between us and marveled at how minty the kiss was without a hint of morning breath from him. He must be magic.

Tracing his thumb across my cheek, he gazed at me for

a moment before he said, "We have to check out in two hours. Do you want to just drive home, or would you like to explore the town a little?"

"If you're not in a rush to get home, let's explore. Do you ever go antiquing?" He nodded in response. "When I researched the town, I discovered they have a slew of antique stores not too far from here. Maybe we could stop at a few along the way home? If you don't mind following me."

"Sounds like fun to me." He glanced down at his watch. "Breakfast ends in a few minutes. Let's run downstairs and grab some before we pack up to go," Manny suggested.

"Did you take off my bra?"

"I was never wearing your bra," he teased. And then he replied, "I thought it would make you more comfortable to sleep. But all I did was unhook the back and you pretty much did the rest in your sleep. I didn't remove your shirt or see anything."

"I just couldn't remember doing it. I trust you. If I didn't, I wouldn't have shared a bed with you." I only wished I remembered his hands inside my shirt removing my bra. The thought alone heated the space between us.

"Did you have nightmares last night? You kicked me at one point, and I wasn't sure if I did something to deserve it." *Fuck.*

"Sort of. Not anything scary really, just insecurity-type dreams." After the last few months together, Manny had become used to my uncertainties. He'd even learned how to react to them for the most part. Instead of questioning my reasoning, he tried to soothe my concerns with logic or with something to make me laugh.

"Like being at school naked?" he asked.

"You just wanted to think of me naked."

"Guilty as charged." He grinned.

Things were going good with us, and I didn't want to freak him out by telling him how insecure I was about us. *Could I call us an us?* I supposed since we were planning a few trips together it was safe; then again, he went on a long road trip with Marie, and they were just friends. Geez, my mind went to so many stupid places so quickly.

"Talk to me, beautiful, what's going on in that brain?" he asked after my brief silence.

"Are we an *us*?" My question stunned him. It was easy to deduce based on the way his eyes widened and his head popped back a bit in surprise. I started to fumble back from the question when he surprised me.

"Of course. I mean, I hope you think so too. I definitely consider us an *us*." He pushed a strand of hair behind my ear, and I leaned into his touch. "Have I made you think otherwise?"

"No. I just wanted to be sure."

"I'm sure enough to cover both of us," he said with a grin. Yep, I was in love with this man, but I had no clue how to express it to him. My only hope was he felt the same way and would say it first. Even if he did, I prayed I had the courage to say it too.

We spent a few hours running around different antique stores in town before eventually kissing goodbye and heading home on our own. The moment he pulled away, I started to cry. I wasn't sure what came over me, maybe just the emotion of coming to terms with my feelings for him or my fear of getting my heart broken. Sobs wracked my chest. I let out a wail of frustration as the pain stabbed at me. Everything about the past few days spilled out in a sea of tears flowing down my cheeks. I pulled over to the side of the road as it became harder to see. With my head against the steering wheel, I tried to catch my breath, to reel in the panic I'd unleashed.

When I got home, I went inside and went straight to bed. The past few days had completely exhausted me.

***

Three days after the trip, Manny and I went on another date. He'd been working extra hours at work on a special project and finally had a little time off. We had our usual dinner with conversation and then went back to my place.

I expected a full make-out session on the couch, per the norm, but instead he wanted to start tracking down events for me, well *us*, to attend.

There was a Facebook group specifically for listing book events. We joined, and I searched the cities. Two hours later, with his help, I'd booked signings in Nashville and Chattanooga, Tennessee; Montgomery, Alabama; and Louisville, Kentucky.

Most of the destinations were a good drive away, but

Manny wanted to try and get several near Marie so she could come up with Constance.

"Are you sure you can travel this much with me?" I asked him many times.

Each time he responded the same way. "It's fine. I make my own schedules, and I'll work over to meet deadlines before we go. It'll be fine. Trust me."

I did. Implicitly.

Chapter Seventeen

MANNY

Scheduling signings with Perry excited me. I enjoyed the idea of traveling, but even more so, the idea of all the time we'd spend together, plus I'd get the added bonus of seeing little Constance some more. *Win, win, win.*

I pulled the phone away from my ear as Marie tried to deafen me with her shrieking. "I guess you're going to be happy to see me, then?"

She laughed. "I'm so excited, Manny. Constance is talking so much now she's even more fun to be around."

"She's always been fun to be around in my opinion, but I get what you mean." Marie had decided to be a stay-at-home mom until Constance started school. Practically being my own boss, it didn't matter if I got texted during the day, so she constantly sent me updates or called me to give her some adult interaction. Since she wasn't working, Jayce worked longer hours, so most days were spent with a nonverbal child. At least these days, she had things to brag about like the latest word her baby girl picked up.

Marie cursed, and then said, "Great. Constance just said, 'Shit.' Jayce is going to love that."

Everything in me said not to laugh, but I couldn't help myself. "Babies are cute when they curse. Don't sweat it, chica."

"Easy for you to say." She changed the subject abruptly. "Will Perry mind if Jayce and I come for the signing? I don't want to make her uncomfortable."

"I asked her the same thing. She said the more friendly faces she sees, the more at ease she becomes." Perry insisted it was fine for me to schedule where Marie could come. One thing I loved about her was she didn't bullshit me. If she didn't want to do something or it made her uneasy, she told me flat out. She didn't beat around the bush or try to soothe my feelings by sugarcoating anything. She was never cruel in what she said. There's a distinct difference in brutal honesty and honesty.

Nothing about Connie... *shit*... Perry was brutal. That was the first time I'd mixed up their names. Even in my head, it could be a dangerous habit to start. I'd never hidden my feelings from Perry about Connie, but I didn't want her to ever think she wasn't measuring up to Connie. Not that I ever compared them more than just in observation; it didn't affect my feelings.

And I knew I had feelings for Perry that had ventured into the realm of love, but I wasn't ready to say it out loud. Part of me still felt as though I were betraying Connie in some way, though I knew in my head I wasn't. My heart hadn't come to the same conclusion.

"Marie, I think I'm falling for Perry pretty hard."

Marie's voice cracked as she said, "That's great, Manny."

"I feel good but also crappy. I miss Connie a lot. I can't stop myself from thinking about her all the time. The only time I don't think about her is when I'm around Perry. I don't know what to make of that."

"Sounds like love to me." She was right. At least I had no better word to describe it. "You should tell her."

"I'm not sure if I'm ready."

"You may never be sure, but when the moment's right, you'll know. Once it's out and you can't take it back, you might find yourself thinking of Connie less."

"I'm not sure I'm ready for that either. It's been almost three years. By now, I figure we would have been married and have had a baby of our own or at least be trying for one, a lot."

"You can't focus on the what ifs, Manny. She's gone, and that future is too. I don't mean to sound cruel, but I want you to be happy. Holding onto old memories will just make you lonely. I want more for you. And Connie did too."

"Damn, woman, when did you get so smart with this stuff? Our roles seem to have switched on us."

"I learned from the best," she quipped. "Oh shoot, I have to go. Constance just woke up. I'll call you later. Love you, Manny Banany," she teased.

I rolled my eyes and huffed. "You're lucky I love you too, Mo."

***

Perry hated to be surprised. I knew this, and yet I did it anyway. I knocked on her door, heard shuffling and then it grew quiet for a moment.

"What are you doing here?" she called out through the closed door.

"I wanted to see you. I brought ice cream!" I held up the pint of rocky road, her favorite, in front of the peephole in the door.

The door creaked open, and when I stepped inside, she was nowhere to be seen. "Where did you go?"

From the back of her place, I heard her call out, "Be right out."

Her laptop sat on the kitchen table with several notebooks next to it, a bowl of trail mix, and a glass of coffee. I'd interrupted her while she was writing. When she stepped out of the back room, I felt an ache in my chest. She had on a pair of pajama pants and a *Walking Dead* themed shirt that read "Look at the flowers or eat your cookies, you decide." Which was about as close to the outfit Connie was wearing the first time I met her as anyone could get. Was this another sign? Or did it mean I needed to slow down a little?

With a smile on her face, she hugged my neck. "I'm sorry. I wasn't dressed before. I just had on a tank and panties." My body responded to the image her words put in my head. Our lips met, and I tugged her closer, wanting more. She moaned against my mouth, and I ground my hips into hers letting her know I wanted her.

"We should slow down," I stated unconvincingly.

"No, we shouldn't." She lifted her shirt over her head revealing a plain black bra and gave me a little shove until I fell onto the couch behind me. Straddling my waist, she moved against my crotch, making it harder to take things slower. We'd waited so long for this already, I didn't know why I kept putting it off. Through her actions, she let me know she was ready to take the next step.

Her mouth traveled to my neck as I slid my hands over the smooth skin of her back. "I love you," I whispered against her ear. She froze in place, and suddenly I was scared to death she didn't feel the same.

"You do?" she asked, sounding surprised. "I…" She couldn't or wouldn't finish her sentence, so I placed my hand on her cheek to soothe her. She leaned against my palm and closed her eyes.

"You don't have to say it until you're ready. And if you don't feel it, then I'll understand. No pressure, Perry. For me it just felt like the right moment to tell you."

"Do you mean it? Or is it so I'll have sex with you?"

"Wow. That's not the question I expected." I dropped my hand to my lap. "So, rewind a moment and pretend I hadn't said it. Would we have continued making out and made our way to the bedroom?"

"That was the plan," she stated matter-of-factly.

"Then why would I feel the need to say those words to get in your pants?" I lifted her off me and stood up. "I probably should go." Of all the ways I'd pictured confessing my feelings to her, I never imagined her response to be an accusation of dishonesty.

"Please don't go, Manny," she begged. Her hand was around my wrist as she pulled me toward her. "I'm sorry. I just wasn't expecting it and didn't know how to respond. I have a hard time trusting people."

Easing my wrist out of her hold, I said, "I know. At some point though, you have to. I meant what I said about how I feel, but I think we need a little bit of a break, so you can figure out what you want from this." I pointed a finger against my chest and then pointed at her.

I heard her begin to cry as I walked out the door. All the strength I had went into not turning back to comfort her. I had to let her go for now. If she took a few days to figure things out, she'd be back, at least I hoped she would. For the moment, I sulked all the way home like a scolded child. Downtrodden, heart sore, and a little frustrated.

There was one place I enjoyed going to blow off steam and that was the gym. I called Brady to meet me there, and we took turns throwing punches and spotting each other with the punching bag.

"What's got you stressed out?" Brady inquired.

"I don't want to talk about it," I stated with a harder punch to the bag. He nodded in understanding and remained quiet for a few minutes while I continued taking out my frustration.

"How are things with Perry?" he asked. To which my response was to hit the bag harder. He bobbed his head up and down. "Ah, I see."

Throwing another hard punch, I knocked him back a

step or two, and he shook his head. "Women. Can't live with them. Wish I was gay sometimes."

I smirked and cocked my eyebrow at him. "Guys have just as many issues. You'd never make it as gay either."

"Touché," he commented with a nod. "I'm thinking of proposing," Brady said, making me lose my step and fall forward with the next punch hitting him straight in the gut. "Fuck!" he called out as he bent over with the wind knocked out of him. "I thought you'd be happy about it," he croaked.

"I am, you caught me off guard though. How are you going to do it?"

"Not sure. I have a ring."

"Stop. Not *that* ring?" Brady had bought a ring for Marie when she was trying to decide who to be with. He was sure she'd pick him, but unfortunately for him he was wrong.

"Dude, how stupid do you think I am?" When I raised an eyebrow and cocked my head to the side, he added, "Don't answer that after all. I traded Marie's ring in for a down payment on Dawn's. You don't think there's bad juju in that, do you?"

"That's pushing it. But as long as it isn't the same ring neither woman will ever know." After a brief pause, I added, "I'm certainly never mentioning it."

"So, I know usually I let you stew about whatever's bothering you, but lately Dawn has us working on our communication, so I'm going to use some tactics on you."

I rolled my eyes and stepped away from the punching bag. "No, you're not. We're dudes, not lovers. That's between the two of you to work on."

"I suppose trying to woo you with my sexy charms won't work like it does on her."

"Not if you don't even buy me dinner first." I sighed and gave in. "I told Perry I loved her."

"That's awesome man, right?" Brady asked, stepping up to take over the punching duties. He stopped, obviously noting the expression on my face. "Oh… she broke up with you because of it?"

"No." Taking a towel from the shelf, I wiped the excess sweat from my skin while Brady waited patiently for my explanation.

"She didn't say it back?" he guessed.

"Nope." Shifting my feet, I stared at the floor. "She accused me of telling her that to simply get in her pants. She didn't believe me." Deep down I knew it had to do with her issues with insecurity, but the more I thought about her reaction, the more it hurt me inside.

"Damn. That's harsh." Brady grabbed a towel to clean up, and we headed to the locker room to change before we left. After we took our showers and got dressed to leave, I was putting my stuff in the car when I felt Brady's hand on my shoulder.

"Look, man, I know you feel like crap, but she's probably just scared. If she really thought you'd lie to her about something so important, then that means she doesn't know you at all." He had a point. Perhaps Perry and I didn't know each other as well as we thought we did.

"Do you feel like grabbing a beer with me? Or is Dawn waiting on you?"

Brady checked his watch. "She won't be home for a couple hours. She had a few late appointments tonight. Lead the way, man."

Pulling into the parking lot of the Ludington Pub, I parked toward the back. When we went inside, I ordered a couple of beers and an appetizer for us while Brady grabbed a table.

"You're back," the young girl behind the bar remarked. She was the one I mistakenly thought resembled Connie when I came with Perry. I'd seen her a couple of times since that day and never saw the resemblance again.

"Yep" was the only thing I could come up with to say as I took the beers from her. "We're over there." I pointed toward Brady who waved.

"I'll bring your appetizer right out and get your order if you want something else." I'd ordered us pretzel sticks and beer cheese.

"Maybe you should ask her out," Brady suggested when I arrived at the table.

"Dude. I just told you I'm in love with Perry, who sort of rejected me, and you want me to just turn around and start dating again? What happened to the hopeless romantic I used to know?"

"Just a suggestion. Don't get defensive. Seriously though, I think Perry will come around."

"Let's change the subject, please." I could talk about all this until I was blue in the face, and it wouldn't change anything about what happened.

"If you could have any super power in the world, what

would it be?" Brady's question would seem out of blue, but that's how we rolled. When all else failed, we turned to pop culture references.

"You've asked this one before, and the answer is still the same. I want to have no fear." Ever since I lost Connie, fear was plentiful in my life. "Being invisible would suck because I don't want to see people act the way they do when no one is around. For the most part, I'm sure I'd be fine, but there would be those people who were either completely hateful or downright disgusting."

"What about super strength? Or the ability to fly?" Those were always Brady's two choices when we brought this up. He never could decide which one he'd want more.

"I think I'm going to change my answer to teleportation. Now that would be a useful power. No more traffic, no crazy drivers to deal with, no airport security checks. Yep, that's my choice."

"That would really come in handy when you start traveling with Perry," Brady said and then cursed under his breath. "Sorry, I didn't mean to bring her up again."

"It's fine. We'll work this out," I said, not adding the extra thought of *I hope*.

"Can I run my proposal idea by you? Or do you not feel like talking about that stuff?" Brady asked with caution in his tone.

"Man, I'm so happy for you having found Dawn. She's an amazing woman. So, yes, I want to know your idea." Dawn had brought so much life back into Brady after Marie dumped him that I owed her a lot. She gave me back my best friend. For months after the breakup, he moped around his house, wouldn't answer my calls, and missed a lot of work. Once Dawn came into his life, he became my best friend again. The guy I grew up with, my brother in every sense of the word other than genetic.

"So, I was thinking of a flash mob," he began. I held up my hand to stop him. "What?"

"Way overdone. It's cute and all, but it's been done too many times now. What else do you have?" By the look on Brady's face, the sheer terrified confusion, he had no plan B.

"I have an idea," I offered. The relief in Brady was obvious by the way his shoulders deflated in front of me. "You know it doesn't have to be flashy. I know a guy who literally stepped out of the shower and proposed to his girlfriend. She thought he was joking, and then said yes when he told her he wasn't. They've been married thirteen years so far so that seemed to go over just fine."

"So, K-I-S-S? Keep it simple, stupid? Is that your suggestion?" Brady asked, nodding along to show his agreement with the idea.

"You work from home, and she usually calls you when she's on the way home from work. What is the first thing you guys do?"

"Usually she takes a hot bubble bath while I cook dinner."

"So, when you're ready, run her bath with the bubbles and leave the ring on the side of the tub, in the box of course, so it doesn't fall down the drain. I predict she finds the ring, stands there for a moment in shock, then comes running out to see what it's about. When she gets out there, you'll be down on one knee ready to propose."

"Damn, dude, that's perfect."

My phone dinged with a text from Perry.

Perry: Can you come over? I want to talk.

Me: I'm out with Brady.

"Hey, man, I need to cut this short. Perry wants to talk. Shit." I looked down to see she'd responded before I could.

Perry: OK, sorry to bother you.

Me: No bother, sweetheart. I was just checking with him to see when Dawn would be home.

"You want to hang out another hour? Perry wants to talk, and I need a little more courage." Brady nodded so I relayed the message to Perry.

Me: Can I come over in about an hour?

Perry: Sure. I'll be here.

Me: See you soon, sweetheart.

I wasn't entirely sure what she wanted to talk about. It hadn't been long since we spoke. Was she ready to break up with me for real or tell me she was scared? The possibilities were many, and I knew it wasn't healthy to stress over them.

Brady ordered us another round of beers, and we sat talking about stupid stuff for the next hour. He glanced at his watch. "It's time to go. You told Perry you'd be there in a few minutes."

I sighed. "Wish me luck." I called for a cab and would let Perry drive me home or call Dawn later if needed. I only had a couple of beers and felt fine, but I never drove intoxicated.

I texted Perry to let her know I had to wait on the taxi and she sent me back a thumbs up.

About twenty minutes later, I arrived at her house and knocked on the door. She called out, "It's open."

Once inside, I glanced around the room taking notice of the romantic scene laid out for me. My hope of this going well shot through the roof. The table was set with two lit candles, a bottle of wine, and two empty plates.

"Are you expecting company?" I teased when Perry entered the room. She blushed as she stepped forward carrying something which smelled amazing.

"I hope you came hungry. I know you were just with Brady, so if you're not…"

"I'm starving," I admitted. Truth be known, I was always hungry. My metabolism was fiercely high.

Once she set the food on the table, I noticed it was a casserole of sorts. She turned to face me and jumped back a bit to find me right behind her. "Sorry, I didn't mean to startle you."

Carefully stepping closer again, she draped her arms over my shoulders, so I placed my hands on her hips. "I'm sorry about earlier. When I get upset, I tend to cook. I made a Mexican lasagna and thought that I could invite you over to apologize instead of sitting here and eating the entire thing myself."

I chuckled and leaned down to kiss her cheek. "I'm glad you did. And don't apologize. Just tell me you took the time to think things over."

"I don't need to. I know how I feel about you, Manny,

and it scares me. No, scare isn't a strong enough word; it terrifies me." She started to move her arms, and I placed my hands on them to stop her. As she relaxed against me, I felt her take a deep breath in. "If you're not ready to say it, I understand, Perry. I'll wait. I'm pretty patient like that." Her body shook gently with laughter. "It doesn't change how I feel about you. I love you, and I meant it. No matter how many times I say it, I'm not trying to pressure you into anything. I just believe in expressing my feelings. I learned the hard way that life is entirely too short to hold back how we feel about someone."

Perry peered up at me and asked, "Connie?" as though it were a question, even when I knew she already had the answer. "I would have liked to have met her. After hearing Marie talk about her, I imagine she was quite fun to be around."

"You two would've gotten along well." I paused. Perry had asked me a lot of questions about Connie before, and I was still unsure whether us talking about her was good for the relationship.

Somehow, she knew exactly what I was thinking. "I don't mind you talking about her. I'm not threatened by her memory, and I know how important she was in your life."

Her green eyes sparkled with the truth behind her words. I leaned in for a kiss and was pleasantly surprised when she met me halfway. My tongue grazed hers, and as she moaned, her stomach growled at the same time. I chuckled against her lips and said, "Let's have dinner."

"I didn't step on your toes by doing something romantic,

did I?" she asked as I pulled the chair out for her to sit.

"No, I think it's great. There's a lot of pressure put on men to be romantic, and we like to be wooed a little too." I winked at her and took my seat across the table. "Well, I do at least." She scooped out a healthy serving and placed it on my plate for me. Next to the casserole was a bottle of wine. Using the corkscrew she'd left out, I popped the cork and poured us each a glass.

"This looks amazing, Perry." Inhaling the scent, I could tell it was just the right degree of spicy. She'd used tortillas instead of noodles and spiced it up with Mexican cheese and taco seasoning on the meat.

With the first bite I sighed in contentment. "Tastes even better than it smells."

She grinned, looking utterly pleased with her accomplishment. The night was going so much better than I'd expected it to go when I saw her text earlier that evening.

Chapter Eighteen

PERRY

After Manny confessed his feelings for me, I was flabbergasted; that's the best word I could use to describe how I felt. My dumbass self opened my mouth and inserted my foot when I accused him of lying.

When he walked out, I curled up into a ball on the couch as hiccupping sobs shook my body. I was sure I'd never see him again. I'd ruined yet another great thing in my life. Every time things started to go well for me, whether it was a job or a friendship, I found a way to screw it up. I pushed people away when the fear took over. When the thoughts clouded my mind so much I could no longer see reality, I ran. Alone was the way I was meant to spend my life.

After drowning in my sorrows for a while, I got online to promote my latest book and envy other people's lives for a bit. As I perused the different social medias, I came across several quotes that seemed to be directed at me. Basically, a lot of "shit or get off the pot."

Every quote I saw was about taking chances in life, carpe-ing the diem, grabbing for love before it got away, and so on. So, I decided a grand gesture was needed. I had a character in one of my books who insisted grand gestures were the best method for any romance pick-me-up. I took a page out of my own book, so to speak.

Knowing Manny was of Hispanic origin, I went with a Mexican lasagna. I found everything I needed, ran to the store, and bought the ingredients, all before texting him to see if he'd come by. If he'd turned me down, I would've drowned my sorrows in food alone.

Luckily my plan went off without a hitch. I expected him to be rude or unkind when he arrived, not that he was ever that way, but some people could be when you rejected them. I hadn't officially rejected Manny, but I was pretty sure he felt I had.

When he told me he loved me, I wanted to jump up and down and shout from the rooftops, but my insecurities rose to the surface, and I acted like an ass instead.

I loved Manny, I was positive of that, but my mouth couldn't form the words yet. More than anything, I was upset about hurting him; but also, I'd been waiting to make love to him for months, and I ruined the moment when we were about to finally take our relationship to the next step. My goal was to get back to that. To show him, with my actions, how much he meant to me.

When he knocked on the door, my nerves frazzled immediately. Sweat pooled around my neck and hairline. Tremors of uncertainty, mixed with a little regret, rocked my body. I tiptoe ran into the kitchen and yelled from that room for him to come in, so it didn't seem like I'd been waiting on him.

I pretended as though I'd been waiting on the food to finish, which was why I didn't open the door, when in reality it had been done and sitting on warm in the oven.

I sprinkled fresh cheese over the top and watched it melt as I carried it into the living room to greet him.

Watching him enjoy each bite of food made me more nervous about what I needed to tell him. In my mind, I feared that saying it out loud would make him tell me he made a mistake before. Irrational as it was, I worried he would admit it was all to get in my pants. Voicing these concerns out loud would sound crazy even to me, but safe in the recesses of my mind, they seemed logical. I hated this daily internal battle.

Besides confessing my feelings, I'd planned to seduce him, which added to the cloud of questions in my mind. Underneath my clothes, I'd donned the perfect set of lingerie. A set I'd bought shortly after we started dating just to be used with Manny. I worried whether he'd think it wasn't sexy enough. Would he laugh at my attempt at romance? Again, none of these were typical reactions from Manny, but I couldn't stop the ideas from forming.

Letting out a groan, he sat back and placed his hands on his stomach. "I'm stuffed." Guiltily, he looked down at his stomach, and said, "I'm going to have to work that off tomorrow."

"Or we could work it off tonight?" I suggested. Before he'd arrived, I'd taken a shot or two of vodka for liquid courage, and it seemed to work. I watched as the lust filled his eyes at my comment.

As a sly grin covered his face, he said, "Sounds more fun than the gym."

Picking up where we left off earlier, I moved over to the chair and straddled his lap. He brushed his fingers through my hair and whispered, "You're so beautiful."

I corrected my mistake from before by not responding to him with words, but with my actions instead. I ground against his lap and my lips vibrated as he moaned against my mouth.

The heat between my legs was building as I felt him grow beneath me. I wasn't a virgin, but it had been a while since I'd been with anyone. His right hand reached up to cup my breast through my shirt while he placed his left hand on my butt, urging me forward as I rocked. His thumb teased my nipple through the thin cotton material.

Our kiss became more frantic as the passion rose between us. I'd waited a long time to be with this man. He stood from the chair, lifting me with him, and dropped my butt on the table in front of where we'd been sitting. His mouth moved down my neck, and the hand that had cupped my breast inched under the hem of my shirt.

The warmth of his hands against my skin made the temperature in the room rise. I wanted him. In one swift movement, I pulled my shirt over my head to allow him better access. His eyes glazed over with passion as he looked approvingly at my sexy lingerie.

He thrust his hips forward against my core, and I placed my hands on his ass to pull him closer still. "Let's take this to my room," I whispered in his ear.

"Lead the way," he growled. I hopped off the table still wearing a bra and jeans. Leaving my shirt on the floor, I grabbed his hand and tugged him in the direction of my bedroom.

As we reached the door, he pulled me back, pressed me up against the doorframe, and lifted my arms above my head. Holding my arms in place, he trailed his tongue down my neck, over my collarbone, and down to the swell of my breasts. My knees weakened with every inch his tongue covered.

"Keep your hands there," he ordered as he let go so his hands could remove my pants. The anticipation of what was to come was driving me wild. The slow agony of him moving the zipper down and then lowering my jeans made me pant anxiously.

I lifted my feet from each pants leg as he removed them and moved back up my body. I wanted his mouth to stop midway up, but he came straight to my lips instead.

"Did you wear these for me?" he mumbled against my lips, his fingers tugging at the waistband of my panties letting me know what he meant. They were dark crimson lace to match the bra with tiny black silk bows on each hip and in between my breasts.

"I bought them for you," I whispered. "I saved them for tonight."

He grinned approvingly and dropped to his knees. Placing one finger on either side of the band, he tugged gently, sliding them slowly down my thighs, over my knees, and letting them fall at my feet. Before I could step out of them, he began to kiss my thighs.

My hands fell to his shoulders, as I was unable to stand with weakened knees. I pressed my fingers through his hair just as his mouth moved from my thigh up to my core. I let out a moan with his name as his tongue worked its magic.

Standing became more difficult by the minute, but I wasn't ready for him to stop. Either he sensed my need, or he wanted to further things along. He stopped, stood up, and tugged me toward the bed. Giving me a light push, I fell onto the mattress with a grin on my face as he stared down at me.

Gently pushing my thighs apart, he went back to work pleasing me. Damn, I loved this man and his magical touch. As his tongue worked at my clit, his hands massaged my hips. My fingers ran through his hair, tugging at strands when he hit that perfect rhythm making my toes curl.

Before I knew what was happening, my hips lifted off the bed and my body shook in a fierce mind-blowing orgasm. Manny crawled onto the bed, pulling himself up until our faces were inches apart. Leaning down, he captured my lips and I tasted myself on his tongue. The moment was intimate and strange at the same time. I'd never had someone kiss me after doing that. Of course, I'd never had someone give me an orgasm during oral sex either.

Wrapping his arms around me, he rolled over, pulling

me on top of him. I sat up, and his hands moved to my breasts, massaging them as I reached behind me to remove my bra. He sat up, keeping me on his lap, and teased a perky bud with his tongue. I thrust against his raging hard-on as his sucking stung the pink tips, causing me indescribable pleasure.

A second wave of release shook my body to the core. Damn, I'd never experienced orgasms so intense before unless it was from my werewolf killer (the silver bullet, my battery-operated boyfriend).

We had yet to even get to the point of penetration, and he'd already given me multiple orgasms. If I hadn't already known I loved that man, I would've been in love with him after that achievement.

Manny reached down and unbuttoned his jeans, lifting his hips to slide them off. I moved off him and helped. His boxer briefs kept his cock from springing forward until I gently rolled them down his hips and freed the monster from its cotton cage.

As I readied to take him in my mouth, he stopped me. "Not this time." He sat up and kissed me. "I want it, trust me. But if I don't get inside you soon, I won't last."

I turned and dropped my butt to the bed, scooting back to display myself in front of him. He crawled between my legs, and in one long, slow movement he pressed inside me. I gasped as his girth stretched my body, and I moaned as he began to move back and forth inside me. Each movement was pure heaven. The thrusts became more forceful and rapid as my next climax approached. My body rocked for the third time just before he cried out with one last strong push.

He collapsed beside me on the bed and pulled me into his arms. Kissing my forehead, he said, "I love you, Perry."

I peered up into his eyes and said the words I felt in my heart, the ones I knew he'd waited patiently for. "I love you."

Genuine bliss, not from the sex, lit up his face. He truly did love me, it was unmistakable. Something my anxiety couldn't take from me.

Chapter Nineteen

Perry fell asleep before I did. I couldn't believe she'd said the words. More than that, I couldn't believe how good they felt to hear. There was a twinge of guilt in my stomach making it hard for me to sleep.

Since Connie died, I'd never experienced intimacy like we'd shared together. Perry and I shared something as deep, if not deeper, than I'd had with Connie. Perhaps it was just different, but I had to admit it felt like a betrayal to Connie's memory in a way.

The feeling of guilt washed away as I stared down at the face of the woman in my arms. She had drifted off to sleep and seemed so content. She fit so perfectly in my arms, nothing about this was a betrayal. If anything, it was unfair to Perry to look at our time together as anything negative.

I wasn't sure how long I watched her sleep, but eventually I drifted off myself. Something jolted me awake, and when my eyes opened, Connie was next to me in bed. I glanced over to see Perry on the other side. Not going to lie, I was sort of hearing the bow-chick-a-wow-wow music playing behind me. Don't judge me, if you had two hot women in bed with you, there'd be dirty thoughts going through your mind too. Or two men, whatever you're into.

Connie shook her head in disbelief. "You're having dirty thoughts, aren't you?"

I chuckled, "Of course not. I'm a gentleman."

"It's the man part that tells me you're lying," she teased. "She's very beautiful."

"So are you," I said, reaching out to stroke my thumb across her cheek. "I miss you."

She glanced over at Perry, and I closed my eyes as the guilt returned. "Don't do that," she whispered. Her fingers grazed my chin as she lifted my face up so our eyes met. "Don't feel guilty. If I could be here with you, I would. But I've been here with you, and I see how happy you've been since she came into your life. You're in love with her?" She posed the question even though she knew the answer. I knew she did because this had to just be my subconscious talking. Connie was gone.

"I do. It's different though."

She placed her thumb against my lips. "Stop. Manny. She's perfect for you. If I could be with you, I would; but if I could make you a perfect match, someone who complements you as equally as you do them, it would be Perry. She's got an amazing heart. And she's crazy about you."

"She's more closed off than you were. Sometimes I have trouble getting her to believe what we have is real."

Relationships came with enough uncertainties, but with Perry those were doubled by her own demons.

"She believes it. And I think she's worth the work."

"I think so too," I admitted. "But if I'm so in love with her, why do I keep seeing you and thinking about you even when I'm with her?"

"I hope it's because you'll always think of me in some way. It's time for closure though. We need to say goodbye to each other for now. I love you, but I can't stay around. If I do, you'll never have the life with her you want and need."

Sitting up, I reached for her and my hand drifted through her chest. She was no longer corporeal. "I'm not ready for you to go."

"We had our time together. Now is your time with Perry. Hold her close; forever is shorter than you think."

And as soon as her words ended, I woke up. What did that mean, forever is shorter than you think? Was that a warning about Perry? Was she sick like Connie?

She stirred next to me in the bed, and I pulled her close, kissing her forehead. Fear coursed through me as I wondered if I'd have to grieve another woman I loved. I wasn't sure I could handle it twice.

Chapter Twenty

Manny's grip tightened around me as though he were trying to hold on for dear life. I'd felt him kiss my head, and I thought he'd been awake, but as I glanced up, I noticed his eyes were shut and wondered if he was having a bad dream.

My dream had been weird. I was at Mount Rushmore staring up at the carvings in the mountain, and a girl with a pixie-cut hairstyle sat on the ground next to me. "Is this your first time here?" she asked.

"Yep, I'm not really sure how I got here either." There hadn't been many places I'd traveled in my life, and Mount Rushmore wasn't a place I'd ever imagined going.

"I saw it first with my best friend, Marie, and I keep coming back here. I think because it was the last stop we had on our road trip." The words Marie and road trip caught my attention, but I still didn't understand this dream.

"He truly loves you, I hope you know that."

"Who?" I asked, not sure what this young woman was

talking about.

"Manny. You don't have to be afraid of losing him. He's got a huge heart, but he's scared of having it broken again. Even with that fear, he's let you in, and he wants to spend his life with you." How did she know all this? As I stared at her, she placed her hand on my shoulder and smiled. "Trust me. I didn't get a lot of time with him, but I can see how happy you make him. Don't hurt him and don't be afraid to love him."

"I won't. Well, I'll try not to at least."

"He's patient, and he'll be a wonderful father." Her eyes skimmed over me, stopping on my stomach, and she nodded.

I bolted up in bed and startled Manny awake. "What's the matter?" He searched the room quickly before his eyes landed on me.

"We didn't use a condom," I stated. The realization had jolted me awake abruptly.

"You're right. That was pretty reckless. I've been tested though. Don't worry." He patted my leg comfortingly.

"I'm pregnant."

Manny laughed and asked, "What? The chances of that are slim, I'm sure. Aren't you on birth control?"

"No. I haven't dated anyone in years, and I've always used condoms for birth control." The girl's words repeated in my head. *He'll be a wonderful father*. The familiar ache of despair gripped my chest.

"Sweetheart, calm down. You're freaking out. It'll be fine."

"She told me. She said you'd be a wonderful father." I was in full panic mode. My forehead beaded with sweat, tremors rolled through my body, and my voice cracked with each word I spoke. If I trusted this woman so much, why didn't I trust when she said Manny would always be there for me?

Before I knew what was happening, Manny had his arms around me, and suddenly I realized the crazy noises I'd heard were coming from me. I was sobbing against his chest, my tears coating his skin.

"Shh," he whispered against my ear. "Sweetheart, everything is going to be fine. I love you."

His words filled me with relief. I'd heard him say them before, but I needed the reminder. I began to deflate, letting myself relax against his body. His presence had amazing healing powers for me.

"Do you want to get out of here for a bit? Maybe go for a drive or something to clear your head?"

Out in public was not where I wanted to be right that moment. "Can we just lie here for a bit?"

With a warm smile, he lay back on the bed and held his arms out for me to join him. I found comfort in the warmth of his embrace, safety in his arms, a feeling of security, a feeling of home. After a few moments, the panic inside me settled. The thoughts normally spinning through my mind had quieted. Manny gave me a little peace of mind.

After the initial shock wore off, I realized how silly I'd been in freaking out over a dream. Connie and I had never met, so if she were a ghost, why would she visit me—

especially when I'm in bed with the man she loved—to tell me I'm carrying his baby. The whole thing sounded more ludicrous each time I thought it. My subconscious was probably just freaking out when it realized no condom had been used.

The next morning, I told Manny all about the dream, without describing the woman completely, and he again reassured me that no matter what, everything would be fine.

Over the next few weeks Manny and I grew closer than ever. We began hanging out with Dawn and Brady more. Being around another loving couple opened up my affectionate side. I would grab for Manny's hand when we were walking. The first few times I did it, he appeared surprised but after a while he grew accustomed to how I'd warmed to him. After a month had gone by, I discovered my cycle was late and the dream came flooding back. I ran to the grocery store, bought a double pack of pregnancy tests, and went straight into the bathroom at the store and peed on the first stick. A few minutes later it came back negative. I sat in the bathroom stall and cried in relief.

The next morning, I peed on the second stick, just to be sure, and that time it was positive. "What the fuck?" How could this be possible? Immediately I went to pick up my phone to call and tell Manny, but I stopped. I had two tests with two different results. I needed to have a professional test. I called my doctor's office and scheduled a visit for later in the week.

Each time Manny called me to ask me to do something, I made up an excuse about deadlines or headaches, whatever it took to avoid seeing him. I wanted to wait until I knew for sure if I was pregnant before I made him worry or scared him away.

The doctor gave me news I hadn't been expecting. "You're not pregnant; however, I think there may be something else going on with you. We need to run a few tests to see what we can find out."

"Worst-case scenario?"

He smiled. "Perry, you always think the worst-case scenario is going to be your fate. So instead of me stressing you out by telling you what it could be, let's find out what it is. Sound good?"

"Sure. But you're positive I'm not pregnant?" Honestly, anything was better than having a baby on the way right now. Manny and I hadn't had enough time together yet for us to bring a child into the picture. Selfishly I wanted more alone time with him.

"I tested it twice and both were negative."

The next week of my life would consist of nothing but tests. I called to tell Manny what was happening. He offered to be there for me at every appointment, but I turned him down because I didn't want to be a burden to him. But I told him it was because I would be better off on my own so he wasn't bored the whole time.

After a bit of coaxing, he agreed to let me go alone. If it ended up being something serious, I'd need him a lot more in the future. The first test was a pelvic exam, which immediately resulted in an ultrasound. The entire time she stared at the screen with concern etched in her features.

After many long hours of tests, I was told I'd hear something in a few days. I barely got any rest. No writing was done because I was too busy staring at the phone just waiting for the call to come in. When the results finally came back, I wanted to be pregnant.

The diagnosis was ovarian cancer, stage two.

Chapter Twenty-one

MANNY

The moment I saw Perry's number on the screen, my chest ached with worry. She was supposed to get her test results soon. "Hey, baby, how are you?"

Her voice cracked with emotion as she replied, "It's ovarian cancer." Two words I dreaded to hear. I almost dropped the phone in shock. I wanted to fall to my knees and ask what the fuck I did to deserve losing two amazing women so young to such horrible diseases. I had to stay positive though, she could survive. I needed to believe it.

"What did the doctor say?"

"A lot of stuff. It's treatable, they caught it early. Of course, my mind instantly retains the factors of making sure it doesn't spread, the possibility I'll never have children of my own, death."

"I'm coming over there." I started to hang up, so she wouldn't have the chance to tell me no, when she surprised me with her response of "Be careful on the way over but hurry. I need you right now."

My chest swelled with pride at hearing the words "I need you." The same words concerned me, knowing how scared Perry must be, since I was filled with fear for her.

In the car, I let my mind start to wander. I slammed my fist against the steering wheel and cried out, "Damnit, Connie! Why didn't you tell me this up front? I can't lose her. It would be like losing you all over again."

No answer. Since the night Perry and I slept together, I hadn't seen Connie again. In a way it was good, but right now I needed a friend. I pushed the hands-free button on the steering wheel. "Call Mo."

"Hey, Manny Banany," she teased.

"Perry has ovarian cancer," I said in a deadpan voice.

"Shit" was all Marie said before becoming silent for a moment. Across the expansive miles of phone lines and states between us, we both sat unable to find any words to cope with this moment.

"I don't know what to say," Marie finally offered up a moment later.

"You're about as equipped to deal with this as I am, then. I know I sound like a selfish prick by thinking 'why me,' but how can this happen twice?"

"Whoa, wait. First off, you're the most unselfish person I've ever known in my life. And second, did the doctor say it's hopeless?"

"No, he said they caught it early."

"Then get off the phone with me and go see Perry. You hug her, tell her you love her, and ask her what she needs.

All that matters now is taking care of her." Damn, I'd taught her well on this tough-love crap.

"What if it's fatal?"

"Then you do the same thing you did with Connie, and you make every minute of your time together count."

"I love you, Mo."

"I love you too, Manny. Now go be with that beautiful woman of yours. She needs you right now more than anything."

"I'm on my way there now. I just needed a little pep talk along the way." We said our usual goodbyes and hung up.

A few moments later, I found myself sitting outside Perry's home. I stared at the door wondering if I could be strong enough to get her through this. I took a deep breath in and released it slowly.

Walking up the short path to her door felt like the road to Mordor, the home of evil in *The Lord of the Rings*. Before I could knock, she swung the door open and flung her arms around my neck. Her body trembled, but she didn't sob, just held me tightly until I felt her relax.

"Hey, beautiful. Tell me what you need from me." She peered up at me with her big green eyes and smiled.

"Can we watch a movie or just sit on the couch? I don't want to talk about anything." She watched me, seemingly to gauge my reaction.

"I don't mind at all." She already had a movie picked out on Netflix, a cutesy teen romance called *The Kissing Booth*. I enjoyed my action films and tough guy flicks, but I wasn't opposed to the occasional chick flick too. Marie and

I watched several at hotels when we were on the road.

The movie was actually pretty good. Perry had relaxed into my arms early on, cuddling up against me with her head on my shoulder and her knees pulled up underneath her. One hand rested on my chest and the other was behind me across the back of the sofa.

When she first suggested the movie, I never expected to be able to concentrate on anything except her diagnosis and treatments to come.

I ran my fingers through her hair and kissed her forehead. When the movie ended, I whispered, "Are you ready to talk?"

She sat up and bit her lip as she shook her head. "Tell me something about you instead. Tell me about your family."

"Have you ever heard of Operation Pedro Pan that happened in the sixties?" She shook her head, which was not an uncommon response when I brought it up to people.

"It's part of my family's history. It's how I ended up growing up in America instead of Cuba. Between 1960 and 1962, Cuban children were being sent to Miami to escape Castro's regime. Their parents weren't allowed to come with them, so the Catholic church arranged for foster families."

"How have I never heard about this?" Perry moved closer on the couch, propping her elbow on the armrest and her head in her hand as she listened intently.

"Many people haven't. If my family hadn't lived it, I might not know about it. My mom was one of the children who was sent over here. A Catholic family took her in. Their priest approached the mother of a family, her name was

Jessa, but I call her grandma. She took my mother in even though she already had four children of her own. The priest said to her, 'You already have four children, you won't notice one more.'"

The most beautiful sound came from Perry's mouth, a laugh. There'd been so much fear and uncertainty in her eyes since I'd arrived tonight, I was glad to see her take a moment to laugh.

"My grandfather wasn't so sure he was ready to take in a little brown baby because, well, it was the sixties and that was a much different time than now."

She shuffled her feet around a bit to get more comfortable and remained completely enthralled in my story. "So, my mom came here at age ten with twenty-five dollars and a visa. And the family, which is now my family, took her in and loved her as one of their own." I was one of the darkest members of my family, but they never even acted as though they saw any difference in our skin tones.

"What about her biological parents? Did she ever see them again?"

"Sadly, no. Her father had been killed years before that, when she was only three. Her mother… my mom says she died of a broken heart. She had a heart attack a few years later and never made it to the States to reclaim her."

"Wow. I don't even know what to say. Do you keep in touch with your family?"

"I do. My parents moved to Florida about five years ago. They couldn't handle the Michigan cold anymore. Most of my mom's family still lives in Michigan somewhere.

They're spread out over the state. I have three aunts, an uncle, and about forty cousins. Catholics have an aversion to birth control, you know."

Perry grew silent, and I wished I'd kept my mouth shut. "It's weird wishing I'd been pregnant instead, considering how badly I was dreading the pregnancy test result." She chuckled, trying to pretend as though she wasn't hurting. I knew better.

Pushing my fingers through her hair, I watched as her eyes closed at the feel of my touch. I palmed the back of her head and pulled her forward until our lips met. Her lips were soft against mine, gently caressing, silently urging for more as she tugged at my shirt. "Stay tonight?"

"There's no place I'd rather be." She took my hand, and I followed her to the bedroom.

Chapter Twenty-Two

PERRY

Manny fell asleep before I did, which was fine. I stared at him as he slept. Creepy, sure, but I didn't care. I wanted to memorize every inch of him. Forever was never promised to anyone. All anyone could do was make the best of the time they had, and I swore to myself I would do that. Even if the doctor said there was no sign of cancer anymore and he could predict the future and know I'd live to be ninety-five, I'd still want to live each day to the fullest.

And I wanted each of those days to start with Manny right beside me. No one had ever made me feel so at ease with a simple look. No one had ever taken the time to find out what I needed instead of insisting on what they needed from me.

Most nights I didn't get much sleep. A normal night for me consisted of anguishing over old conversations, or future conversations, or things that had never happened but could. I wished I could be like the stories you read in books or see in movies where the person can't sleep, and suddenly they fall in love, and being next to that person gives them the ability to relax enough to rest. It never came that easy to me.

"Can't sleep?" Manny's voice scared the shit out of me. I jumped up and slammed my hand against his chest in the process. "Shit," he exclaimed as he sat up and grabbed his chest in pain.

"I'm sorry," I said just before smacking my hand over my mouth.

"It's fine, sweetheart." He grunted, rubbing the spot I'd hit. I hoped he wouldn't be bruised in the morning. "Too much on your mind?"

"Maybe?"

"My mind is always on high alert, even if everything is going my way, which doesn't happen very often." Manny rolled onto his side and propped his head up with his hand. "I know you don't want to talk about anything serious, so just talk about whatever is on your mind," he suggested. "Or tell me a little about your family."

"My family is nowhere near as interesting as yours." How could I follow up a tale of being ripped from your family and sent to live with strangers because the leader of your country was a horrible person?

"No competition. I just want to know where you came from."

"I was born and raised in Michigan. My parents are good people. They live in Florida now too, oddly enough. I moved there with them for a while before coming back to Michigan. The crowded cities of Florida were too much for me." I paused, wondering how much I should tell him. "They're a little smothering. I get my anxiety from my dad's side. I think my mom helped him come out of his shell quite a bit." On the surface, my dad seemed outgoing, but there were times, when we were in a crowd together, where I saw the signs: tense shoulders, subtly looking for an exit, tight jaw, sweating.

"How did they meet?"

"College. She was best friends with his sister."

"Was that weird for your aunt?"

"She's the one who thought they'd be great together." I always thought it was strange that my aunt would set up her brother with her best friend, but the older I got the more it seemed to make sense to me.

"That's pretty awesome."

"They're great parents; I couldn't ask for better. I need to go visit them more often than I do. As much as I enjoy my alone time, the thought of traveling so far by myself scares me." I took a road trip once from Michigan to Florida, over twenty hours, and the interaction with people along the way and the nerves I felt for the entire length of the trip exhausted me to the point where I slept my first two days there.

My dad had anxiety issues a lot like mine. The difference between us was I accepted mine and found ways to cope with it, while he ignored it and occasionally suffered panic attacks that he blamed on anyone around him. My dad's a decent man, but he's in denial.

"Now you don't have to travel alone. Why not look for a signing in Florida, or just plan a trip, and I'll go with you?"

Manny wanted to meet my parents? I'd never introduced anyone to them before. The thought never occurred to me. No one had ever been special enough, but Manny was different. Manny was amazing. "Unless you don't want me to meet them?" he asked, my silence obviously alarming to him.

"I'd love for them to meet you," I stated honestly. I knew without a doubt they would adore Manny almost as much as I did. "We'll plan a trip soon." Biting my lower lip, I lowered my gaze from him. "I probably should tell them I'm dating you first."

Manny laughed. "That would be important." His forehead crinkled with worry. "I know you don't want to talk about it, but did the doctor say anything about treatment?"

I knew I couldn't avoid the subject forever. "She wants to start soon. I asked her to give me some time to get through these signings and then we could begin. I just need a few weeks of happiness with you. Does that make me crazy?"

"Not at all. It makes you pretty much human." He embraced me and kissed my forehead, an action I always found to be sweeter than any other gesture a man could make to show he loved a woman.

* * *

Manny arrived at seven to pick me up for our first signing trip. Michigan in October usually stayed in the fifties or sixties, so I dressed somewhat warm. We were headed into

Tennessee, and based on what Marie said, I needed to bring both shorts and jeans because they never knew what the weather would be like. She even said there were days where I would wake up and want jeans and then change later in the day. Weather like that made packing increasingly more difficult.

"Are you bringing everything you own?" Manny asked as he stepped out of his vehicle. He ran up to help me as I struggled to get down the stairs with two rollaway bags, a toiletry bag, and a carry-on for the front seat so I could stay busy. My carry-on contained my nifty writing thingy, my iPad full of downloaded Netflix movies, an iPod, and my Kindle. If I got bored on this trip, it would only be because my batteries died… on everything.

"I blame Marie. Because of her, I had to pack a week's worth of clothes to cover all four seasons." I pointed up at the top of the steps. "And my books are still up there. You sure you don't want to rent a minivan?"

"Brady's let me borrow his SUV. I cleaned out the trunk and made room in the backseat, so we got this. I even filled a cooler with Cherry Coke Zero for you." Taking one of my bags first, he leaned down and gave me a kiss. "I hope you're ready for this. Marie wants to do some double dates while we're there. She's also agreed to come to the signing and help me with being the bringer of sales. We're going to pimp your books. We have matching T-shirts."

I started laughing until I realized he wasn't joking. "What do the shirts look like?"

"Mine says, 'Back off. I have a crazy author girlfriend

and I'm not afraid to use her,' and Mo's says, 'I'm with stupid.'"

Just as I was about to freak out a bit, Manny cracked a smile and gave me a wink. "No worries, chica. They have your author logo on them, and the back has your name and the titles of your series and the genres you write. They're very tasteful. We both just want to draw attention to your amazing work."

"You're both awesome, and I don't deserve either of you." For years, I pushed people away when they got too close to me. Since the day I met Dawn and then Manny, I'd done my best to hang onto these amazing people. None of them had a clue how important they'd become to me. And now Marie, someone who barely knew me, was supporting me unconditionally. I wasn't sure what to make of everything changing in my life.

Manny loaded the SUV. Though there was no room for anyone else to ride along until we could unload the car, he could still see out the back window, so it wasn't totally overflowing. There was even still a little room to buy a few things along the way if we wanted. And if I was lucky enough to sell out of books, there would be even more room.

We had a ten-hour drive in front of us. I buckled in. Manny would drive the first hour or two. He arranged the seat, put the car in drive, and placed one hand on the wheel and one on my upper thigh. My skin tingled any time he touched me.

"What do you want to do first when we get to Nashville?" The drive would be long, but we left early enough in the morning, so we could get there at a decent time.

"See Marie of course." Placing my hand over his, I said, "I know how much you miss her and Constance. As long as we get there at a decent time, before the baby goes to sleep, then we could hang out for a bit."

"Marie will be tickled pink." He gave a little laugh and asked, "What does that mean anyway? Where do these sayings come from?"

"I never understood them either. I google a lot of old sayings I use in my writings. I'm sure we'll hear a lot of great ones in Nashville. Hasn't Marie ever used anything crazy around you?"

Manny snorted. "Marie tries her best not to speak in country sayings. She told me once her grandmother used to say, 'I feel like everybody's eat' after having a big meal." Besides the bad grammar of the phrase, I wasn't even sure what it meant. "And they eat sort of weird stuff there sometimes too. Gravy on everything, sweet tea… *really* sweet tea. The first time I had Southern sweet tea, I thought I would slide into a diabetic coma."

His description was not entirely off base. I'd had sweet tea before down south, and it was nothing like sweetened tea up north. "I've tried it." I yawned and covered my mouth.

"If you want to sleep, go ahead. I'm going to drive for a few hours at least." I felt his hand brush the hair behind my ear as I drifted off with my head against the window.

A few hours later, I woke up to an empty car. The car doors were locked. I checked my surroundings and determined I was at a truck stop. I wasn't sure what state we were in though.

Me: Where are you?"

Manny: Sorry, sweetheart. I had to make a pit stop. I'll be out shortly, getting some high-octane coffee so I can stay awake.

Me: Grab me a 5-hour energy?

Manny: Yes, ma'am.

Five-hour energy drinks kept me alert through many deadlines when the exhaustion started to set in. They didn't cost much, and I couldn't drink them often, but they certainly worked for at least four to five hours, or it was a great placebo if nothing else.

I stepped outside to stretch my legs. The moment I stood up, I realized I had to pee. Manny came out of the store a moment later. I waved and yelled, "my turn," and ran past him into the store. The ladies room had a line, as most do, so I stood and did the pee-pee dance for the next few minutes and released Niagara Falls when I finally made it to the toilet.

"Ahhhh," I sighed audibly. The woman in the next stall laughed.

"Long drive?"

"I think so. Where am I?" I flushed and stepped out of the stall. "My boyfriend is driving, and I was asleep." After speaking, I considered whether or not I'd referred to Manny as my boyfriend before. I couldn't remember ever saying it.

"You're around Fort Wayne, Indiana. Where are you headed?" We made small talk as we washed our hands. She had a husband and three kids in the car, and they were on their way to Kentucky to visit in-laws. When I mentioned I was an author, she showed genuine interest. I gave her my business card, and she promised to download and review my series.

As I walked outside, it dawned on me that we'd talked for a while. Manny probably thought I either fell in or—the worse thing for a new girlfriend to reveal—that I had pooped.

Manny stood with his back against the car, his arms across his chest, and one leg crossed over the other. With his hair lightly blowing in the breeze, sunglasses on his face, he looked like a model from a book cover.

"I was talking to a woman in the bathroom." Manny nodded in understanding and instead of leaving it at that I added, "Didn't want you to think I was pooping or something."

Manny let out a loud laugh. "Everybody poops, hun."

"I did notice a fabulous T-shirt on my way out the door. It was a cat wearing a cowboy hat riding a unicorn through space." Each detail of the shirt made Manny's eyes grow larger along with the grin on his face.

"Tell me you bought it," he commanded.

Pulling the shirt from behind my back, I said, "I stole it." His mouth dropped open in shock. "I'm kidding! I totally bought it for you." As I held the shirt up, he snatched it from my hands and waved it in the air.

"I freaking love it." He tossed me the keys. "Let's get on the road."

Once we were back on the interstate, I got up to speed

and stuck the car on cruise control. "Your turn to take a nap."

"I can't nap in the car. Besides, I want to keep you company."

I snorted. "Gee, thanks. Now I feel bad for snoring and most likely drooling while you were driving."

"First of all, you were definitely drooling. And second, I didn't mind. I just can't sleep when the car is moving." His phone buzzed. "I called Marie while you were in there, and she said that she wants us to come by, no matter what time. Her parents have Constance for the night, so we won't see her, but she and Jayce want to feed us and maybe play a few games."

"Sounds great." I kept my focus on the road. Staring ahead, I zoned out a bit as I worried about how our evening would go. *Would I act like an idiot in front of Jayce and Marie, or would I be comfortable around them?* My chest tightened with each thought, and my left leg shook with nerves.

"Stop." Manny placed his palm on my thigh. I looked around, unsure of what he meant. We were flying down the road at almost eighty miles an hour, so there was no stopping.

"What do you mean?"

"I know what's going on in that beautiful head of yours. Stop overthinking it." Before I could argue with him, he said, "I know it's not that easy, but try. If it helps, Mo and Jayce both think you're awesome."

"What can I say? You bring out the best in me." That was

no line of crap. Everything came easier with Manny in my life. Occasionally I found myself even communicating with strangers, like the woman in the bathroom at the truck stop.

"I promise to try to relax." That wasn't about to happen, thanks to my mom. My phone rang. "Hey, Mom," I answered. She'd called me from her cell phone for a change, so I knew this time it was her.

As I greeted her, Manny said something about the GPS. "Honey, who was that?"

"Mom, I'm driving. I can't really talk." Manny's hand slipped over mine. He slid the phone free. My eyes widened in fear of what he was going to do. A second later my mom's voice called out, "Sweetie, are you there?" Instead of taking over the call as I feared he would, he turned the speakerphone on for me.

"I'm here." I glanced over at Manny. "Say hi to my friend Manny, Mom."

"Friend?" she asked with heavy curiosity.

"Boyfriend. We've been seeing each other for a few months. He's traveling to a signing with me this weekend." Manny eyed me questioningly. I nodded approval for him to speak, not that he needed it, but I appreciated him waiting for my signal.

"Hi, Mrs. Jordan. I asked Perry to bring me down to Florida soon. My parents live in the state as well." Throwing me a wink, he continued. "Your daughter is amazing, if you don't know already."

"I do know. I'm glad to see others are noticing too." I could hear the amusement in her voice. Before I knew it, I'd be getting emails regarding weddings. "I'm pleased to meet you, at least by phone, Manny."

"The pleasure is all mine." I saw him punch something on the phone. "Does she know about your diagnosis?" I thought my eyes would pop out of my head. "Relax, I muted the phone to ask. Mrs. Jordan?" No answer. "Mrs. Jordan, excuse me while your daughter and I have sex." No answer again, thankfully. "See, she can't hear."

"You better be damn glad she can't. And no. I'm not telling her yet." The more people who knew, the more real everything became. And until I knew my chances, until I'd done a few treatments, I didn't want my parents to worry.

"Hello? Are you still there?"

Manny hit the mute button to return to the call. "We're still here. We went through a bit of a bad spot. Do you mind if we call you later?"

"Sure, you two have fun and be safe please."

After we said our goodbyes, Manny hung up the phone. "Your mom is sweet. I'm surprised you told her about me."

"I should've done it a long time ago. Who knows how long I have left," I teased.

Manny didn't appreciate the joke at all. His jaw tensed. "Please don't joke about dying."

"Sorry." The next bit of the drive was a little awkward as the terrible joke hung over our heads. He didn't stay quiet for too long though.

Chapter Twenty-Three

MANNY

Asking Perry to stop worrying was like asking a fireman to ignore a fire alarm. When her mom called, it took her mind off other things for a few minutes. And then things became awkward after her bad-taste joke. During the two hours she drove, I tried to keep her mind off the pending social events. It seemed to work until we were about an hour from Nashville.

Since I knew the best way to get to Marie's house, we pulled over and changed places. She glanced at the time and her leg started to bounce. One hand tugged at the hem of her shirt and the other picked at lint on her jeans. The anxiety had started to settle in. We'd been together long enough for me to recognize the signs.

"If it would make you more comfortable, I'll call Mo and tell her we're too tired and we'll see her in the morning."

"I'm fine," she stated firmly.

"Are you…?"

"Yep," she answered before I could ask again. Another thing I'd learned was not to over ask with Perry.

When I knew we were only five minutes away, I pulled over into a parking lot. Perry glanced around nervously. "Wh-what are w-we doing?"

"Tell me five things you can see around you."

"What?"

"Just go with this. Tell me five things you can see around you," I repeated.

"A Target store, cars, a woman picking a wedgie out of her butt, a used diaper, and a Wendy's restaurant."

"Now name four things you can touch around you," I said, using a calming tone in my voice.

"The steering wheel, the gear shifter, my cup of water, and you," she said with a warm smile.

"Three things you hear," I urged her on.

"Carole King on the radio, laughter from across the way, and a motorcycle going by."

"Two things you can smell?"

She inhaled deeply. "Your cologne." Then she said, "The remnants of our snack earlier."

"And finally, something you can taste," I added.

She leaned forward and pressed her lips to mine. After a moment, she whispered against my lips, "You." With her forehead pressed against mine, she said, "I love you for learning anxiety exercises."

"You knew that one?" She nodded. "I want you to have fun this week, and I'll do anything I can to make it easier for you."

"You really are the most amazing man ever." She buckled her seatbelt back up, after she had released it to lean into the kiss. "Let's go see Marie."

Marie must've been eagerly awaiting our arrival because before we'd turned the car off she was out the door hobbling toward me as quickly as she could. She rammed into my arms and planted kisses all over my face. "Jesus, woman. How much caffeine have you had while waiting up for us?"

Laughing, she lowered her arms and said, "Not a drop if you can believe it. I give up caffeine when I'm pregnant. Jayce took Constance to my parents' house and hasn't gotten back yet, so all my pent-up energy is yours."

"Lucky us," I called out to Perry who looked a bit scared of Marie. I couldn't blame her.

"Hey, Perry." Marie dropped it down a notch or a hundred for Perry, thankfully. "Do you mind if I hug you?"

"As long as you don't jump on me or kiss my face," she joked. Marie crossed her finger over her heart in an X formation. Eyeing Perry's face as Marie leaned in, I didn't see any anxiety or panic arise. She appeared calm.

Marie wrapped her arm around Perry's shoulder and led her inside, grabbing my hand and pulling me along at the same time. "Are you two hungry? We can order pizza. Or I can call Jayce and have him pick up some burgers or Chinese. What are you guys in the mood for?"

"We haven't eaten a real meal in several hours, so even a cardboard box sounds delicious," I said, exaggerating slightly.

"Chinese sounds amazing. I'd like to treat if you don't

mind," Perry offered.

"That's so sweet, thank you," Marie stated without arguing. Knowing her the way I did, it drove Marie nuts to let someone else pay. She accepted the offer, knowing Perry wanted a way to connect. "I'll call Jayce. Do you have any favorites? We can just get a few different things and share?"

"Sesame chicken, crab rangoons, lo mein, it all sounds delicious," I offered my two cents on the topic. "I could eat a box of each."

Marie turned to Perry. "He's not kidding. When we were on the road, this guy ate everything in sight. One night he finished off an entire pizza by himself. He's a bottomless pit."

"I know. The first time I made him meatloaf, I thought I made too much, but there was nothing left over." I stayed quiet and let Marie and Perry bond. I'd never seen Perry talking so freely to someone she barely knew. Either she was at the peak of nervousness and rambling, or the calming exercise in the car worked better than I expected.

"I need a good meatloaf recipe. It's Jayce's favorite main course, and I know he only eats mine because he loves me. It's terrible. It's basically meat and ketchup." Damn I felt old sitting around listening to these two swap recipes.

"I make mine with barbecue sauce, and instead of bread crumbs, I use Stove Top mix. It's basically the same thing with some great seasoning mixed in," Perry opened her phone and started looking through her photos. "I got it off the back of a Stove Top box and took a picture of the recipe so I wouldn't forget it."

"Text it to me." The girls exchanged numbers and talked for a few more minutes about different foods they both loved. I watched Perry closely, hoping she wouldn't shut down in the middle of their conversation. I'd seen it happen when her anxiety caught up to her brain and threw in a dose of panic.

Marie glanced down at her phone. "I'm going to shoot Jayce a text real quick and tell him we're calling in an order for him to pick up. My little way of telling him that Constance will be fine and he can come home already."

"Bit overprotective, is he?" Perry snickered at Marie's exaggerated eye roll and nod of agreement. "Imagine when she begins dating."

"I dread it for Constance more than anything. He's going to be the 'standing at the front door holding a shotgun' kind of dad. He doesn't even care for guns, but he'll still do it just for effect."

"I imagine Manny will be like that one day too. I'm pretty sure he'll even stand by Jayce when Constance starts dating." Perry and Marie turned my way and started laughing when I nodded and grinned.

Perry continued. I realized she was stuck in a ramble when she said, "Our kids will never know what hit them when they start dating." And I saw the moment her brain caught up to her mouth. Her eyes widened, and her words stuck in her throat with her mouth hanging open.

"Can I use the restroom?" she squeaked.

"Sure, it's just down the hall. Second door to the left."

Perry sprinted down the hall, and Marie's eyebrows rose

in my direction. "She spooked herself with talk of your kids. That sounds pretty serious."

"No kidding. We've never talked about marriage or kids or anything." We'd said our I love yous and implied our intentions for a future together.

"How did it make you feel to hear it? Did it scare you?" Marie whispered, glancing down the hall to check for Perry.

"Not at all. In fact, I thought it was pretty awesome. Perry would be an amazing mom. Jude loves her. We've been having him over a lot, and he always gets very excited to see her." Marie clapped her hands together, grinning like a freaking Cheshire cat.

"Calm yourself, Mo. I should probably go check on her."

Marie grabbed my wrist and stopped me. "Give her a minute."

Chapter Twenty-Four

PERRY

Things had been going well. My mouth worked long enough for me to have a normal conversation with Marie, and then my brain had to butt in.

Manny and I had never talked about kids or marriage or anything of the sort. And I just blurted the words "our kids" as though it was a normal thing to say.

Leaning against the wall, I laid my head back and pouted. "Why do I have to be so panicky about everything?"

I needed to walk around and gather my courage to go back in the room. Though the house was a decent size, there were only a few rooms in the back where I could stay out of sight.

Not wanting to be intrusive by going into bedrooms without permission, I moved toward a shelf at the end of the hall with pictures on it. On the top shelf were pictures of Jayce and Marie at their wedding and a picture of them the day Constance was born.

And then my eyes landed on a picture of Manny with a girl. The girl I'd seen in my dreams, the pixie-haired girl who told me he'd be a great dad. "How did I know what she looked like?" I asked the question out loud but didn't expect an answer since I was alone.

I picked up the photo and stared at it. Their heads were pressed together, they were both smiling, and their eyes were closed. Most likely the cutest picture I'd ever seen. Even with their eyes closed, you could see the chemistry burning between them. *How could I ever match up to her?*

"You don't have to compete with her, you know." Marie walked toward me. I set the picture down where I found it.

"Sorry, I didn't mean to…." I didn't know what I was about to apologize for. I simply looked at a photo on display in her hallway. It wasn't as though I had rifled through her underwear drawer to find a secret stash. Why does my mind indulge such weird thoughts?

"They were really happy?" I meant it as a statement, but it came out with inflection as a question.

"They were. And I've never seen him as happy as he was with her." She placed her hand on my shoulder and added, "Until you."

"Yeah, right."

"I have no reason to lie. I like you, Perry, and I want us to be great friends. Right now though, Manny is one of the most important people in my life, and if I didn't think you were good for him, I would tell you in a heartbeat."

"I met her."

"Constance?" Her forehead crinkled with curiosity.

"Where? When?"

"You're going to think I'm crazy. It was a dream. I didn't know it was her until I saw this picture."

"Manny sees her too. I never believed in ghosts or much of an afterlife until she passed." Marie opened the bedroom door next to where we stood and motioned me inside. "Have a seat. I told Manny we were going to have a little girl talk, and Jayce will be home any minute."

The room was decorated in comic book characters, mostly Marvel but with a bit of DC mixed in—well Batman was represented at least. "Is this your room?"

"The guest room. I told Manny before I came back here that I'd like you two to stay here for a few days if you want."

"I'd love to. I love this room." Nerd was in my blood. Flowers and color-coordinated rooms never appealed to me. The more I looked around, the more I noticed. There were bits of *Harry Potter* mixed in and even a little of *The Walking Dead*. "I feel at home here."

She smiled warmly, obviously appreciating the sentiment. "That's why we decorated it this way. All our favorite genres are in here, and it's the room we reserve for those most important to us."

"I can see why Manny loves you guys so much." Things were going well until I stuck my foot in my mouth with the next comment. "He told me once he wished you lived in Michigan too, said it made him wish you'd chosen Brady a little bit." I cringed and apologized immediately for bringing him up.

Placing her hand on her swollen belly, Marie closed

her eyes. "Don't apologize. I know you meant no harm."

"My mouth runs faster than my brain sometimes." I dropped my eyes to the floor, avoiding eye contact with her as my heart began to race. Internally, I couldn't stop going over the idiotic comment. I fidgeted with the hem of my shirt.

"I like your honesty. It's refreshing." In a drawer next to the bed, she pulled out a picture from under a book. "This is me with Connie."

"Why do you have it hidden away?"

"Because I miss her. And because Brady took the photo." In the background of the picture, I recognized the New York skyline mostly from the show *Friends* and other TV images.

"I'm jealous of all the places you've been." On the back of the frame, another photo stuck out, and I pulled it through the crack to see it better. "Oh wow. Mount Rushmore. Was it awesome to see in person?"

Taking the picture from my hand, she held it against her heart. "I forgot that was back there. I hid it because it was our last photo ever. She died a few hours later."

"I'm not sure I believe in ghosts, but if I did, I don't understand why she comes to visit me but not you?"

"My guess is that it's because I have everything I need. Jayce, Constance"—she placed her hand on her belly again—"this little guy. She's looking out for Manny's happiness."

She peered over at the door momentarily and then lowered her voice. "Manny said she visits him too, but that he hasn't seen her again since… the time you guys said it."

"He told you about that?" I didn't know whether to be angry or flattered. I supposed if I had a best friend, I'd tell them intimate details of my relationship too.

"It's something we promised Connie that we'd do. We share our happiest moments in life with each other." My embarrassment faded away quickly. Knowing he considered it one of his happiest moments gave me chill bumps.

"He said it's one of the happiest moments?"

"Top ten, no doubt," Manny interjected, standing at the door leaning against the frame. I wasn't sure how long he'd been there and tried to think quickly if I'd said anything to worry about.

"Top ten? Seriously?"

He thought a second and replied, "No, that's not really true. It's top five." My heart sank at first and then soared to the top of cloud eleven. Two steps above cloud nine of happiness.

"Jayce is back, and the food smells so damn good I'm going to eat it all if you ladies don't join us." Marie exited the room, and Manny grasped my wrist, twirled me to him, and planted a long sensual kiss against my lips leaving me both breathless and speechless.

"I love you," he murmured against my lips. "Let's go eat."

He didn't even care that I hadn't said it back. We'd reached the point where he just knew. With a burst of courage, I followed him into the living room and greeted Jayce.

"Hey, Perry, great to see you again," he greeted me back.

"Thank you for dinner, Marie said you treated?"

"I was happy to do it." Jayce glanced down at a text. He grinned so widely it was easy to guess what it was about. "Pictures of Constance?"

"Hmm?" he asked, glancing up at me.

"Is that the text? Pictures of your little girl?"

"Was it that obvious?" I shrugged because it was completely adorable, but I didn't want to say that in case it sounded weird.

"Do you want to see?" The hopeful look in his eyes told me if I said no, he might crumble in disappointment. And, of course, I wanted to see because babies were always adorable.

"Definitely," I replied. He was as excited as a kid who just got permission to go play with his friends. Quickly pulling his phone back out he showed me the picture his parents sent of Constance sleeping peacefully. After I *awwed* enough over the picture, he said, "I have a few others I took earlier today too."

Manny and Marie were setting the table with plates and silverware, and I heard her laughing. "Jayce, Perry doesn't want to see all the pictures of Constance."

"I don't mind at all." Without missing a beat, he continued showing off the pictures of Constance eating ice cream, Constance running around the house in her diaper, and Constance in the bathtub giggling at something that must have been hysterical.

"Dinner is ready," Marie called out, interrupting the slide show.

"Thanks for humoring me. It never seems to get easier to let her go to my parents overnight."

Marie chuckled. "She's only stayed over there twice. Give it at least a few more times before expecting it to get easier."

We passed the small cardboard boxes around the table, scooping out a little from each one for a nice assortment on our plates. The first bite was heaven.

Manny finished his first plate and was asking for seconds before I got halfway through. The man was a human garbage disposal. One couldn't tell by looking at him. His muscles were so defined, and though he didn't have a chiseled six-pack like you see on some models (usually thanks to photoshop or makeup) his chest was perfect. Just soft enough to cuddle on. My imagination had wandered into the sexy zone, and I needed to get out of that mindset.

"Would you guys like me to bring out some wine?" Marie asked.

"No, we're good." I answered for Manny because I knew he wouldn't want to drink when Marie couldn't, what with being preggers and all.

"Perry, I hope it's okay for me to tell you this, but I finished one of your books, and I absolutely loved it."

"Why wouldn't it be okay to tell me that?" I smiled widely. "That's amazing to hear. Now if you'd told me that my story was horrible, the hero was crap, and my heroine was whiney as fuck, then, yes, I'd be offended."

Everyone stared at me for a minute and then broke out into laughter. "Sorry."

"No, don't apologize. You're getting comfortable around us, I like it. Feel free to curse or say what you feel." Marie didn't know what she was saying by giving me the freedom to curse. I put sailors to shame at times when I got started. I always held back when I first met someone to make sure they weren't offended by my language.

"Careful there. I've heard Perry's language when she lets loose." Manny winked at me and I laughed.

"He's not kidding. I was raised in an Irish-Catholic family and curse words are more common than the word *the*." I continued talking without thinking, my usual bad habit. "Brady was shocked the time I let out an F bomb when we were driving to a concert a few weeks ago. He wasn't expecting it and almost drove off the road."

The mention of Brady's name made the room tense. "Sorry. I thought you guys were all friends now."

"No, we are. It's funny." Marie paused and glanced over at Jayce whose jaw was tight. "We had a little disagreement earlier about Brady, that's all."

Jayce's head shot up. "Marie. I don't think they want to hear about it."

Marie scoffed. "Well, you didn't mind the neighbors hearing about it when I asked you to keep your voice down outside. These are our friends, they care about us. It was a simple mistake."

"A mistake? Calling me Brady?" Manny's eyes widened in my direction. One could cut the tension in the room with a chainsaw. Why had I made the mistake of saying his name? Everything was uncomfortable now, which made my anxiety rise.

"Look, you two. I don't know what's going on, but if you need us to leave...."

Marie had tears in her eyes. "No, don't go. I'm hormonal. Earlier, I got a text from you, Manny, and you mentioned Brady. As I was reading it, I called out to Jayce but accidentally said Brady's name instead."

"Why didn't you just tell me?" Jayce inquired.

"Because we went straight into the argument, and then you left to drop Constance off." Jayce walked over to Marie, bent down, and kissed her. Anything was better than listening to them fight.

Manny cleared his throat as the kiss went on a bit longer than it probably should have in front of company. "Get a room, you two."

Marie wiped her mouth as Jayce moved away. "Sorry. My hormones have been all over the place with this pregnancy. So much worse than it was with Constance."

Agreeing with a nod, Jayce said, "We're hoping that means it's a boy this time since things are going differently."

"If it is, then you can name him Manny." Two guesses on who suggested that and the first one doesn't count.

"Or Brady?" I offered as a joke. Their eyes widened, and I asked, "Too soon?" to which they all had a good laugh. That was close. I'd taken quite a chance with a joke like that after the argument they'd had in front of us.

"You're quite funny, Perry." I worried Jayce wouldn't like that joke, but it seemed to be right up his alley.

With a full belly, the exhaustion set in and I yawned,

covering my mouth as it stretched to the fullest. Manny wrapped his arm across my shoulders. "You sleepy, sweetheart?"

"I guess so." I stood up and stretched. "If you want to stay up and hang out, go ahead."

"Are you sure?" I nodded. Addressing Marie and Jayce he said, "I'm going to say goodnight to Perry and I'll be back if you guys feel like hanging out?"

"I'm kind of tired myself, but you and Marie are welcome to catch up. Since you two have a couple of days before the signing, we'll hang out tomorrow."

"Sounds like a plan."

Manny walked me to the guestroom and shut the door. When he leaned down to kiss me good night, I tugged at his T-shirt pulling him closer, wanting him to stay with me just for a little while at least.

My hands slipped underneath the hem of his shirt. He groaned as my fingers grazed over his muscles. "Maybe I should call it a night with you," he said in a hushed tone.

"You can always wake me up later when you come to bed. For now, go hang out with your friend."

"I'll take you up on that offer later," he stated with a kiss to my neck.

Chapter Twenty-Five

MANNY

"I'm sorry for our outburst a moment ago," Marie said the moment I returned to the living room.

"Is everything okay with you two?"

Releasing a deep sigh, she relaxed into the sofa, letting her head fall back against the cushions. "From the outside looking in we're great, but things have been a little tense lately. After finding out Dawn overheard my conversation with you, I filled Jayce in on everything."

"Everything?" A silent nod was all she gave me. "That had to hurt."

"Both of us. But Jayce suffered the most. I've never seen so much pain in his eyes, Manny. No matter how much I tried to convince him that I'm not in love with Brady, he couldn't hear it. He left for three days." This was all news to me.

"What? We talk all the time, Mo. How did this never come up?"

"You've been busy with Perry. Plus, I was ashamed." She craned her neck to peer down the hall. "He cried, Manny. I'd never seen him so vulnerable before. He'd be so embarrassed if he knew I was telling you this."

"Nothing wrong with a man crying. We have emotions too. Since Connie died, I've cried more than I ever thought I could. It's only been recently, I can think of her without getting emotional." Marie patted my leg in a show of comfort. "It may sound cheesy, but Perry has healed me. I never thought it was possible." Checking down the hall myself this time, I went back to the subject I knew Marie needed to vent about. "Can I ask you something?"

"Absolutely."

"Do you think you should cut ties with Brady completely? For your marriage's sake?" The flash of pain in Marie's eyes answered my question. She'd considered the idea and the pain associated with it. "He's going to propose to Dawn." She bit her lip to hold back the emotions. I could've worked it in a little easier, but I felt she needed the reality check.

"What did he do with the ring?"

"Sold it." I knew what she was really asking was the same question I'd posed about Brady using the same ring. "She's good for him, Mo." Leaning in toward her, I lowered my voice to almost a whisper. "Call me selfish, I'd love having my two best friends together for life, but I believe you two ended up where you're meant to be. Now instead of just my two best friends, I also have two very close friends in my life."

"I love Jayce. So why is it so hard to hear that Brady is

getting married?"

"Well, he hasn't proposed yet," I teased. She gave a light chuckle, so it worked momentarily to lighten the mood.

"She'd be an idiot to say no."

"Speaking from experience?" Jayce asked as he walked into the room. "Sorry, I just needed a glass of water." His apology fell short due to the tone of the voice speaking it.

Marie's head dropped in defeat. She sighed, stood up, held up one finger to let me know she'd be back, and disappeared into the kitchen.

"That was awkward," I mumbled to the empty room. While they were gone, I picked up the phone and texted Brady to let him know we'd made it to town and just to check in.

Me: We're staying with Mo for the next few days. We arrived a few hours ago.

Brady: Baby Constance cute as ever?

Me: In pictures. I haven't seen her. She's with Jayce's parents.

Brady: And Jayce and Marie?

Me: Yep, they're cute as ever too.

Brady: Ha ha! Funny.

I considered telling him about the drama currently unfolding in the kitchen, but it wasn't my place to air her dirty laundry, especially to the person dirtying it unintentionally.

Me: They're good.

Brady: Cool. Have fun, man.

Smacking my palm against my forehead, I scolded myself for not being more helpful to my two friends. If I hadn't lost Connie and known the pain two years later with having found love again, I'd have thought they were both holding onto something too tightly. But I understood. Would it be easier for me if Connie were alive and in love with someone else? I wanted to believe I'd be happier with her on earth, but that's easier to say knowing what it felt like with her gone.

My head popped up at a strange sound coming from the other room. A moment later I heard chairs clattering and a low moan. "Shit." I sprinted down the hall to the guest room. I paused and heard more noises coming from the kitchen. I wasn't going to listen to my friends having sex, but I was glad to know they had kissed and made up, literally.

Giving them their time together, I snuck into the guest room to check in on Perry. She was snuggled under the blanket with her arm over the top. Lifting the covers, I slipped underneath. I rested my head atop her shoulder and placed my arm across her stomach. She murmured something and pushed her butt back against me. I started to harden the moment she made contact.

With a brush of my lips against her neck, she rolled over to face me. "Hey, what time is it?"

"A little after eleven. I came to check on you."

"You didn't visit for long," she asked, her eyebrows scrunched together.

"She and Jayce needed a minute."

"Okay," she drew the word out as if she wanted an explanation.

I raised my eyebrows and tilted my head a bit.

Then she nodded and said, "Oh. Got it.... Maybe you could take a break too?" As if she thought I needed her to clarify, her hand moved down under the covers to cup my hardening cock. I groaned as her hand rubbed me through my jeans. Thrusting my hips forward, she unzipped my pants.

"It's my turn to take care of you this time," she whispered against my lips before kissing me. Her head disappeared beneath the covers and I lay back on the pillow. Just as her mouth enveloped me, there was a knock on the door. Perry paused midsuck and the door cracked open.

"Are you going to bed? I didn't mean to leave our conversation." Marie was whispering, assuming Perry had been asleep instead of waiting patiently under the covers with my dick in her mouth.

"No. I came to check on Perry. I'll be back in there in a few minutes. Make us some popcorn, and we'll watch a movie."

"Got it." As soon as the door closed, Perry resumed sucking as though nothing had interrupted. *Fuck, I love this woman.* And not for the sex, but everything about her. I wanted to see her, so I moved the cover away, and the instant I did, our eyes met, and I almost came in that moment. The way her hair cascaded around her face, her green eyes boring into mine; the entire few seconds it lasted were intense.

"Slow down, I'm getting close."

She ignored me and went faster instead. A moment later, I thrust my hips forward and released myself into her mouth. She clamped her lips shut taking it all down her throat. "Shit."

With a smile, she wiped the side of her mouth and moved up next to me. "That was all about you this time. Now go visit with your friend, and we'll continue this later." Our lips met, and after that I didn't want to leave the room. The soft skin of her belly rubbed against mine where our shirts had ridden up. I wanted more contact with her; I was ready for much more. Flipping her over, I ran my nose along her neck breathing in the soft sweet scent of her lotion.

She gasped as I bit down on her earlobe at the same time my hand stroked between her legs. "Manny," she moaned against my ear.

"Do you want me to stop?" I asked.

"No, I want you," she begged.

Answering her plea, I pushed her shirt up and moved my mouth to her nipple. The string of her pajama pants was loose. I tugged on it to untie them and then slipped my hand underneath the hem and into her panties. She was already so wet for me.

"Damn, you're ready for me," I growled.

"I am," she moaned. I grabbed a condom from the dresser and was about to open it when she stopped me. "I want to feel you. I'm on birth control, we don't need that too."

And with that, I pushed inside her, all the way in. When I couldn't get any deeper, I began to move as she wrapped her legs around my waist, grinding her hips in time with mine. Tilting her body just right gave me the angle to go even deeper. Perry threw her head back with pleasure and let out a loud sigh slash moan. Realizing where she was, her eyes widened. She grabbed the pillow next to her and covered her face to suppress the moans. I wanted to see her eyes. I moved the pillow and placed my mouth over hers instead.

Our movements became rhythmical to the point I lost track of everything around me. Afterward, when we were lying on the bed sweaty and panting for air, I saw my phone light up.

Mo: Did you fall asleep?

The light came from a social media notification. Underneath it was a text from Marie sent a half hour before. I responded quickly, wondering if she'd given up on me.

Manny: You still up?

Mo: Just went to bed. You sounded… busy.

Manny: Sorry :/

Mo: No, don't apologize. Tit for tat, right? Lol

Manny: Terrible pun. Lol. Let's catch up tomorrow night?

Mo: For sure. See you in the morning. Love you

Manny: love you, Mo.

Perry nestled up against my chest and started to snore lightly. The soft breaths against my skin gave me goose bumps. I pulled the covers up over us, kissed the top of her head, and allowed myself to drift off to sleep.

***

"Good morning," Perry greeted me the moment my eyes

opened. As they adjusted to the morning sun coming through the window, I tried to focus on her face. Her honey-blonde hair stuck up in different directions, and her peridot eyes were practically glowing.

"Morning. You look happy this morning."

She grinned back at me. "I slept pretty well, didn't you?"

"Best night's sleep in a long time."

"I feel bad you missed time with Marie last night. I'll make sure you two have time to talk tonight." The way she fidgeted with the blanket made me wonder what the deeper meaning was behind her statement. When she worried too much, she fidgeted.

I rolled over and propped my feet on the floor. With my arms over my head and my feet straight out, I stretched and yawned loudly. "You can visit with us you know. She wants to be your friend as well."

"I know, but I also know you two have a history. With that history comes a strong bond, and you need to be able to talk about whatever you want." Again, her words had an ominous meaning behind them. Perhaps her paranoia of worst-case scenario was contagious, and I'd caught it. I probably read too much into her expressions.

"I have no secrets from you."

"Except for the ones where Connie visits you?" The only reason I hadn't mentioned those was because I thought it made me sound crazy.

"Did Mo tell you that?"

"Don't be mad at her. It was in response to me telling her that I've seen Connie in my dreams before." My head spun around so quickly my neck cracked. "That sounded painful."

"It's fine. When did you see her?"

"The night we first made love. She's the one who told me you'd make a wonderful father someday. It's because of her that I took the pregnancy test. She's the reason I found out I have ovarian cancer."

And the harsh reality came crashing back. *Cancer*. I'd gone to sleep and forgotten about Perry's diagnosis for a while.

"I know it sounds silly, but I feel like she's your guardian angel." Perry must have noticed the skepticism in my look. "I'm not a very religious person, I'm the first to admit that, but there was something so real about my dream. I didn't know what she looked like, so how did my subconscious create a person who looked exactly like her?"

"How do you—"

"Marie has a picture of the two of you in the hallway. I can tell how much you love her." The glow left her eyes briefly.

"*Loved* her, she's gone."

"Just because she died doesn't mean your love for her is past tense. I'm not jealous or hurt by it." Running her fingers through her hair, she sighed. "Well, I'm a little jealous. I want the kind of love I saw in that photo."

I opened my mouth to argue, and she stopped me. "I know we could have that, but we're not there, Manny. You've been so good to me, and I'm grateful for the time we've spent—"

"Stop. What are you trying to say?" I stood up, turned around, and bent over with my hands propped against the bed so we were eye level. "Are you breaking up with me?"

"I don't know."

"What does that mean?"

"It means, I have cancer. I may survive it, and I may not, but I don't want to be the second great love of your life to die." She backed away from me, scooting to the other side of the bed. "Before this becomes a great love story, maybe we should just end things while they're good. Give us both some really happy memories."

"That's fucked up, Perry." I slipped my shorts off and went to get in the shower. *Maybe when I get out, she'll have come to terms with how crazy she sounds.*

Once in the shower, I put shampoo in my hair and her words started to sink in. I smacked my hands against the wall, over and over again, and then I screamed out my frustration.

"Manny?" Marie called out. "What happened?"

"Nothing. Sorry, bad morning."

"Perry just left. Did you guys have a fight?" Without a thought, I pulled open the shower curtain and stepped outside with soap in my hair and water all over.

"What the hell do you mean she left?"

Marie covered her eyes and turned away grabbing a towel off the rack next to her. She blindly handed it toward me. "She called a Lyft and took off with her stuff. I thought maybe you two had planned that until I heard how angry you were in here."

Before drying off, I stuck my head under the faucet to remove the excess shampoo. I dried and dressed while Marie followed me around with her eyes shielded. "I'm decent enough now."

"You were pretty decent before, but I'm married," she said with a wink. I wasn't in the mood to laugh. "What happened this morning? Everything seemed so great last night."

"Last night was amazing. Apparently, it's how she wanted it. She's decided she wants us to end on a happy memory before she becomes a great love I end up grieving."

"What the hell?"

"My sentiments exactly. I think she's read too many of these romance novels… or watched too many Hallmark movies… or something… with these women who decided they're going to die on their terms and spare everyone else."

Throwing my clothes around the room, I screamed in frustration once more. Marie wrapped her arms around me. I relaxed into her, squeezing her close to me, needing the comfort.

"She doesn't get it, Mo. Perry doesn't want to become a great love, so she dumped me. What she doesn't understand is I'm already there. I've imagined our future, and it's what I want." The irony was I decided this all last night after she mentioned the possibility of our kids, probably the same moment that made her decide to dump me. In all honesty, I was jumping to conclusions. Perry hadn't officially dumped me, but it felt that way.

"Go after her. She probably went to the hotel where her

signing will be. It's in two days, and I remember her saying she would have to go sign in and get all her information today or tomorrow. Go make a grand gesture." Marie kissed my cheek. "I'll make you some breakfast."

"I'm not hungry."

"This little one is though," Jayce said, walking into the room with Constance in his arms.

"There's my girl." Constance's eyes lit up and her chubby little arms reached out toward me.

"Manny," she squealed. Once she was close, she wrapped her tiny arms around my thick neck and nuzzled her head against my shoulder. Marie told me she'd showed Constance my photo often, but this was the first time I heard her speak my name. The moment was a proud one.

"I missed you, sweetheart." I kissed her head while rubbing her back. She cooed into my ear. "This one makes everything better," I said to them.

"Just like her namesake," Jayce commented.

Closing my eyes, I expected to see Connie walking toward me with her arms extended, but my mind showed me Perry instead. "Baby girl, I'll be back in a bit to hang out with you, deal?"

"Play?" she inquired.

"I'd be honored to play with you in just a little while." As I handed her back over to Marie, I said, "I'll be back. To quote a great movie, I gotta go see about a girl."

Perry's schedule was in my phone. I'd made a copy because I knew how much she liked to be prepared. When it came to stuff she liked to check, doublecheck, and sometimes triple check herself to be sure.

That morning she was due to be at a hotel in Chattanooga to get registered for the signing. I wasn't sure what I'd do when I got there, but I had a few minutes to figure it out.

The Bluetooth was connected to the car so when my phone rang, I had high hopes it was Perry. "Hello, sweetheart?" I answered, hoping to hell it was her.

"Hey, baby, how's it going?" Brady replied. "Since when do you call me sweetheart?"

"I hoped you were Perry. What's up, man?" I'd never been so disappointed to hear Brady's voice before.

"Why don't you tell me first? Why did you hope I was Perry?"

"She got spooked and ran off, man." Spooked was the best word I could use for what happened. Why else would someone end a good, no, a great thing, on the chance something bad could happen?

"Well crap. Okay, go get her."

Before he hung up, I yelled out, "Wait! What did you call for?"

"It's not important. Go find your girl. And call me later."

When we mapped the drive from Marie's house to the hotel, it was only about fifteen minutes away. Driving it now felt longer than getting here from Michigan.

While sitting at a light, I took a chance and sent a text to Perry.

Me: Why did you leave?

Perry: I told you why.

Me: Don't do this. I love you.

Perry: I know. I love you too.

The light changed to green. As I started forward, I sighed in defeat. Her reasoning made no sense whatsoever. One of the things I hated about watching chick flicks was it always seemed the lead, whether female or male, was making some asinine decision that compromised the entire love story. If our story had been a movie, I'd be yelling at the screen right now about the girl being an idiot and needing to turn around and go back to him.

"Life imitates art I suppose." The words came from beside me. I turned to see Perry sitting there in the passenger's seat, and I jerked the wheel in surprise and swerved to the side. I pulled over to gather myself. "You're not real."

"I'm not?" she asked. Taking her index finger and thumb she pinched the skin on her forearm. "Feels real to me."

"I'm losing my fucking mind."

She laughed. "Now that is possible. Why are you seeing me now?" Good question. I wondered the same thing. My mind played tricks on me all the time. "You're stressing too much over me. It's why I left. Do you really want to have to put this much energy into a relationship?" With her head tilted and one eyebrow raised, she stared at me, waiting for an answer.

"You're worth it." Her head jerked back in surprise, lips twitched into a smile, and her eyes filled with tears. "You're my great love, Perry."

Once the hallucination was over, the seat was empty. I merged back onto the road. The hotel was just up ahead on the left. A sign for parking advertised ten dollars for the event. I happily paid it, she was worth it.

The lobby of the hotel was packed with people. I wanted to scream out for Perry but didn't want to embarrass her. I searched the room. Standing near the elevators, away from the crowd, I spotted her. There was fear in her eyes. Fear of the crowd in front of her, the anxiety was eating her alive. I knew she was about to bolt again.

Searching out a path to her, I noticed I could go to the right, slip around the escalators, and come up behind her. That was the route I chose.

As I approached, I heard her frantic breathing, the panic had begun. "Perry," I called out to her. She turned to face me. Holding onto hope, I opened my arms. She flew into them without hesitation. Her entire body trembled. I held her tighter until she relaxed in my embrace.

"You came?" She sounded completely surprised. Why was it so difficult for her to believe I loved her?

"What will it take for you to trust in this thing we have?" I kept my hands on her shoulders but moved back to face her. "On the way over here, I had a conversation with someone."

"Connie?"

"No… you."

Her eyes widened. "You've lost your damn mind!" The comment gave us both the giggles. I jerked her forward again, kissing her forehead. "You really saw me?"

"Yes. I know, I think I've probably got a tumor or I'm schizophrenic… I'm not sure which yet."

"I'm hoping for schizo, then maybe you'll come close to understanding my anxiety thoughts a little better."

Another nice moment of laughter followed her comment.

"Schizo would be nicer than the tumor idea." The crowded room was getting louder by the minute. "Can we go somewhere to talk?"

Glancing at her phone, she replied, "I have a few minutes." She held up her hotel keycard. "I was taking this stuff up to my room. Then I have to go set up my table."

The elevator ride to her room on the tenth floor was spent in silence. As the door slid open, I took control of her luggage cart and followed her to the room. "I didn't think you'd come after me," she said as soon as the door closed behind us.

"Why?" I moved away from the cart, so I could be closer to her. "No matter what the future holds for us, I want to be with you. I want every minute we have left to be spent together. I need you to believe me, to believe in us."

Her eyes glistened with tears. She bit her bottom lip and closed her eyes. After a moment, she took a deep breath, shook her head, and sighed. Her expression suddenly became very stoic.

"Do you remember our second date?" she asked.

"Of course, we had an amazing time." Thinking back to the night under the stars in the gazebo, I tried to understand why she brought it up.

"You said I'd only have to say I don't want to see you anymore, and you would respect my wishes." She peered up at me.

"You didn't say those words exactly," I commented.

"I don't want to be with you anymore," she stated plainly.

"Ouch," I replied. I placed my hand over my chest where I felt a sharp pain suddenly invading my body. A pain I hadn't felt since losing Connie. "Please, Perry."

"You promised." How could I argue with her logic? Telling her how much I cared did nothing to change her mind.

I placed my hand against her cheek, she leaned towards my touch with her eyes closed. "You're right, I did." As much as I hated to do it, I dropped my hand from her face. Turning around, I walked toward the door, looked back one more time hoping for her to beg me to come back. She had a habit of changing her mind abruptly, and I hoped for once it would happen in my favor. The truth was in her expression, her eyes were firmly planted on me, no tears and no pleading were present.

"Goodbye, Perry." Stepping out of the room, walking to the elevator twenty feet away, I thought my body would give out. Yesterday everything between us was perfect. Two people in love, talking about the future, not a care in sight other than being together. At one point in the night, lying there with her in my arms, I came to realize I wanted to marry her. I wanted to wake up next to her every day for the rest of our lives no matter how long either of us may have.

In the blink of an eye, without warning, my whole world had been flipped upside down. My legs suddenly felt so heavy, my feet were planted in place. Every part of my body wanted to stay with Perry, but I had to respect her wishes. I knew she loved me, but I also knew her anxiety was working against us. Her fears were winning. I had no idea how to convince her we'd get through this together stronger. What I couldn't understand was how she could look so cold as I walked away. She showed no emotions, no regret. Could I be wrong about her? Perhaps she didn't love me as much as I thought? Tears welled up in my eyes as I fought back the emotions. Unlike anything I've felt before, the ache in my chest grew stronger. Each step grew tougher.

All my strength went into walking away from the woman I loved.

Chapter Twenty-Six

PERRY

Using Manny's own words against him broke my heart. Once the door was closed, I fell to the floor in tears. My whole world revolved around him. We lived in a small town where we shared friends. I wasn't sure I could avoid him.

When I made the decision to leave him, there was another decision I had to make at the same time. "Hi, Mom," I said into the phone. "I wanted to let you know I've decided to move back closer to you and Dad."

"You know I'll love to have you around, but, sweetie, I thought you were happy in Michigan?"

"I was. I need to tell you something though." Originally, I planned to hold off until my treatments were started, but I needed a support system. All the emotions of losing Manny and dealing with the diagnosis were coming to the surface again. I fought back tears as my voice cracked. "I have stage two ovarian cancer. As soon as I finish the signing this weekend, I start my treatments in Florida. I'm going to need you and Dad to help me through this." I'd been making plans for the last few weeks, just after receiving the diagnosis. I knew the last thing I wanted was to be a burden on Manny, but selfishly I wanted a little more time with him.

"Perry, how long have you known?"

"About a month. I wanted to wait until the next two signings I had registered for were over, but my doctor said I needed to get started before it spread more. She was reluctant to give me this month." All this information was kept from Manny. He'd have never gone to see Marie with me if he'd known. I wanted to give him this trip. I'd planned to break up with him once we were back home, but I changed my mind after our night together. I wanted us to end on a perfect note.

"What about Manny?"

"We weren't serious," I lied.

"Sounded pretty serious on the phone." She called me out on my lie. My mother knew me better than almost anyone.

"Doesn't matter. I just wanted to tell you about my move. I'll call you in a couple of days when I get back to Michigan." I hung up the phone before she could ask any more questions about Manny. Just as I hung up, a text came through.

Marie: Manny is devastated

Me: I'm sorry.

Marie: Don't be sorry, just fix it. He loves you.

Me: I know.

Marie: Do you love him?

I didn't answer for a few minutes, hoping she'd give up.

Instead I got another text.

Marie: Silence is as good as a yes to me. Change your mind, Perry. You'll never find another guy like Manny. He's one in a million.

Marie: You're his great love… his words.

Me: I need to go. Take care of him.

The next text she sent wasn't words but a photo. Marie must've taken it of us. We were sitting in her house, Manny was smiling at me with his hand against my cheek. My eyes were fixed on him. The photo reminded me of the one I saw in Marie's hallway. The amount of love in the photo with Connie was portrayed in this one between us.

I'd made a huge mistake. *Why do I always screw up everything? Will I never be able to have real happiness without questioning or sabotaging it? What's wrong with me?* My legs gave out from beneath me, and I leaned against the chair next to me for support. *I've ruined the best thing that's ever happened to me and there's no going back. How could I be so cruel to such an amazing man? I never deserved him.* Slowly lowering myself into a seated position, I felt the tears streaming down my cheeks. I missed Manny so much already. I wanted to call him, beg him to come back to me. I needed him to forget everything I said about wanting him to leave me alone, the pain I probably caused him by saying it. My chest ached, my knees trembled, and the weight of regret was crushing my heart.

The pain was so intense I couldn't stand it. Sobs racked my chest and I screamed out in frustration, in pain, and in mourning.

Chapter Twenty-Seven

MANNY

Marie knew things went badly the minute I walked into their house. I couldn't say the words, she simply read them on my face. Walking over to the playpen, she grabbed up Constance and brought her to me. "Manny!" Constance cheered as I scooped her into my arms. I held her close enjoying the baby smell, the unconditional love she emitted. Marie grabbed her phone and was texting someone. I assumed it was Jayce. I hoped they weren't fighting again. By the look on her face, the texts were not what she'd expected.

"I probably need to pack and head home since I don't have a reason to be here anymore."

Marie's hand came to rest on my shoulder. "The hell you don't. You're staying here with us. You're always welcome, no matter what."

"Thanks, Mo."

"You were gone most of the day." The words formed a statement, but there were questions buried beneath it.

"I drove to Nashville and back. I needed to think." I hadn't planned on going so far. Pulling out of the hotel, the interstate was in my path, so I took it. I drove two hours thinking about Perry and what I could do to change her mind. When I made the promise to leave her alone if she asked, I had no clue she'd use it against me when things were so perfect between us. In truth, nothing was perfect, ever. We'd come as close to perfect as I'd had in a long time. "I don't know how to get through to her, Mo. I'm fighting an invisible demon determined to keep us apart. No matter how I many times I tell her I love her, she can't hear me. I'm lost at what else to do."

"No hope at all?" Marie hedged around straightforward questions for a change. She wasn't doling out orders for me to chase after the girl anymore. I didn't understand what had changed.

"Maybe. I'll know when we get back home. We live in a small town, she can't avoid me forever." I wouldn't force her to be with me, but maybe I could convince her to change her mind by reminding her how good we were together. "Dawn might get through to her."

"Good idea. You should ask Dawn to help."

"Maybe time apart will help clear her mind? Perhaps she'll figure out all of this was a mistake on her own. For now, I want to spend time with this little one and you." I peppered Constance's cheek with kisses making her giggle.

"She adores you," Marie beamed.

"At least someone does." Her smiled faded with my self-pitying comment. "Sorry, Mo. I'm not the best company, I suppose."

"Oh please, you've been there for me in some of my worst moments. It's what we do." Marie tugged me toward the other room. "I made chocolate chip cookies with pecans."

"My favorite." What I wanted to say was how much she and Dawn were alike as I remembered my first date with Perry, and how Dawn used cookies to bribe me for details.

Marie handed me a cookie first and then bit into one herself. "You know, you can still make a grand gesture at her signing." The thought was one I'd already considered.

***

Two days of hanging out with Marie, Constance, and Jayce worked wonders on my attitude and confidence. The morning of Perry's signing, I awoke with a fresh mind, ready to win back the woman I loved with a grand gesture.

"Good morning, Mo," I greeted her with a kiss on the cheek.

"You're up early this morning. And you're wearing a smile. I like this Manny."

"Me too. I'm going to take your advice and make a grand gesture."

Marie squealed and hugged my neck. "Go get her!"

Joining the line outside the signing, I paid my admission and grabbed the map of authors. Quickly finding Perry on the map, I headed straight for her table. When I arrived, it was empty. "Excuse me, are all the authors not here yet?"

I asked the woman at the table next to her. She shrugged and asked, "Are you looking for someone in particular?"

"Perry Jordan? She was supposed to be sitting here according to the map." I held up the piece of paper as reference.

"I believe she was the one who cancelled last minute. Sorry," she stated. She held up one of her novels. "Would you like to hear about my books instead?"

"I'm in a bit of a hurry, but I'll take your card." I grabbed her business card and stuck it in my pocket. Working my way back through the crowd, I went out the door toward the elevator. Once on the tenth floor, I went to her room, took a deep breath, and finally worked up the courage to knock.

"Just a minute," I heard from inside the room. I smiled to know I hadn't missed her. Until the door opened and a maid stepped out. "Can I help you?"

"I was looking for the woman staying in this room."

"Whoever was in here checked out early this morning. I'm getting it ready for the next occupant." With a quick peek inside, I saw the bed had been stripped, there was no sign of Perry.

"Thanks," I replied.

Defeated, I took the elevator back down, got in my car, and drove back to Marie's house. Once again, my heart had been ripped out of my chest, at least metaphorically, though it hurt as if it were literal. I now knew the answer to what I'd wondered since Connie died. Would it have been easier if she'd dumped me and moved on? The answer was no, the pain of losing Perry was almost as horrible as it was with

Connie's death. The only thing keeping me on my feet was that it wasn't permanent like my situation with Connie. A glimmer of hope was there, even if it was small.

I arrived at Marie's, desperate to see my friend in hopes she could help me through this insanity called life. No one was home. I couldn't sit there and do nothing. I gathered my things and sent Marie a quick text.

Me: Perry's on her way back to Michigan.

Mo: I'm sorry, Manny

Me: What's a grander gesture than driving ten hours?

Mo: Please be careful and let me know when you get home.

Me: Will do.

I considered sending Perry a text, but I was afraid it would spook her more. I attempted to drive the entire trip without stopping, but after five hours, my bladder was about to burst. My body and car were running on fumes. I stopped at a gas station, grabbed a bite to eat, and filled up my tank.

The phone rang, and I connected it to my Bluetooth. "Hello?"

"Hey, man, it's Brady. Where are you?"

"I'm just across the state line. I'll be home in a few hours. I had to leave early, it's a long story." I wasn't sure I could talk about it all yet.

"No worries. Marie called and filled me in on everything. There's something I wanted to tell you the other day, but I didn't know how serious it was until I talked to Marie." My friend called her ex, even though it could damage her marriage, all to protect me. I was a lucky man to have such awesome friends.

"What is it?"

"Dawn is Perry's emergency contact. She received a call the other day from Perry's apartment building because they needed access to her unit in order to check on a possible wiring issue. The landlord preferred to have a witness for the matter. Dawn went over and everything of Perry's was packed in boxes. I thought maybe you two were planning on moving in together and you hadn't told me yet." Suddenly, I realized Perry had planned this breakup in advance. Thinking back, she'd insisted on dragging all her luggage for the trip down to the car. At the time I simply thought she didn't want to be a burden, or wanted to prove her independence, things she worried about often. She didn't want me to see her boxes packed.

"No. Apparently she planned this all on her own. I never saw it coming."

"What are you going to do?" Back before Marie had made her decision about Jayce and Brady, I'd asked him a similar question. His answer had been to propose to her, forcing her hand one way or another. The outcome was not one I wanted to experience for myself.

"I have no idea. I had a plan, but if she is moving, then she must be telling me the truth. She wants this to be over, no exceptions."

"You're going to accept it and move on? Just like that?" Brady's surprise was warranted. I'd never been someone to just give up without a fight. There comes a time in life when even the fight seems futile. As worth it as Perry was, I never wanted to guilt her to be with me.

"I promised her I would. I guess I'm going to keep the promise no matter how much I hate to."

On my way home, I drove by Perry's place against my better judgment. I knocked on the door. If she answered, I didn't know what I'd say. I only knew I wanted a chance to have a proper goodbye, and I wanted her to keep in touch.

No one answered after I knocked several times. I leaned in and peered through the peep hole. I could see enough to know the apartment was empty. She'd already left. I had no clue where she went or if I'd ever see her again. One question I'd always wondered was whether it would have been easier to know Connie was alive even if I couldn't be with her. I knew my answer as it related to Perry, the not knowing was worse.

Life was unpredictable and could end at any moment. Seeing Connie's lifeless body, knowing I'd never be with her again, it broke me. Perry leaving was so much different. I worried if she would get the treatments she needed, if her anxiety would take over making her close herself off from the world. Or worse, would she forget about me and find love with another man? I wanted her to be happy and feel freer, but I wanted all of that to be with me by her side.

Chapter Twenty-Eight

PERRY

The day of my signing, I woke up in such a funk, missing Manny, I decided to cancel. I lost my table fee, disappointed my fans, but I had to do what was in my best interest. I looked into renting a car, but a flight cost only a little more. I wanted to get home as quickly as possible, say my goodbyes, and move on with my life.

Manny wasn't due home for a couple of days. Even if he left the same time I did, he wouldn't make it home for hours due to the long drive. I called Dawn to pick me up from the airport. The moment I got in the car, I knew she was aware of what happened with Manny.

"Your landlord called me to the apartment while you were gone. I saw the boxes."

"I'm moving back home," I blurted. Dawn sighed loudly.

"When do you leave?" she asked.

"As soon as I get home. I hired a mover, and they're going to pick up all the boxes this week. I'm starting the drive home today." Dawn turned into the parking lot of a superstore and put the car in park.

"What about your treatments? Your job? Manny?"

"My treatments start next week in Florida. My job will still be working from home, so I can do that anywhere." I ignored her last question.

"One more answer," she goaded me. I had no answer for her. "Do you know Marie called me today? She asked me to talk to you. Do you know what kind of strength it took for us to talk to each other? We did that for you. We both love you, and we both think you and Manny belong together. Do you want to know how much I believe that?" She waited for me to answer. I sat silent, still. "I believe it enough I asked her to talk to Brady and tell him everything. I put them on the phone together. As insecure as I am about them having any contact, I did that because you're my friend. Your happiness is important to me."

Dawn's sacrifices may seem small to an outsider looking in, but I knew how much she feared Marie taking Brady away from her. Knowing she talked to Marie and then encouraged them to talk to each other spoke volumes about her loyalty to me.

"I know you're scared to be with Manny. I didn't know Connie, but I've heard the stories. I'd be intimidated too. But one thing I've heard above anything else from Manny… he always says the same thing. 'Even if I'd known I'd only have a few months with Connie, I wouldn't have changed a thing. I don't regret the amount of time we had together, a minute of happiness outweighs a lifetime of grief.'"

"Take me home, please."

Dawn didn't argue with me.

I'd miss her almost as much as Manny. She was my first friend in Michigan. She'd brought me to Manny, who gave me some of the best memories I'd ever have in life. *How do I repay her?* By stomping all over her friend's heart. For the last few days I'd picked up the phone several times to call Manny. I'd played through every scenario. In some cases, he'd answer the phone, I'd ask him to forgive me and he'd show up at my door a few minutes later for a long, passionate kiss. On the opposite end of possibilities, he'd tell me I never meant anything to him; it was all about sex, and I did him a favor by leaving. Realistically I knew the second one would never be anything Manny would say to me, but lately my thoughts were rarely logical.

After the cold way I asked him to leave me alone, the pain I watched fill his eyes, I had no right to ask him to forgive me. A huge part of me wanted to run to him, but I couldn't find the courage. Running away was easier to accomplish.

Two hours later, I had packed up my Jeep with everything I could fit inside. I was about to leave everything important to me behind. Everything I'd worked so hard for, relationships, comfort, a sense of home, it would all be in my past. I'd destroyed the happiness I'd always dreamed of finding. Already I sensed the anxiety inside celebrating its victory. I'd let my insecurities and uncertainties take over my life. And after a few minutes of sobbing uncontrollably in the parking lot, I pulled onto the road, prepared to say goodbye to my life in Michigan. Each mile I drove filled my heart with more remorse.

Chapter Twenty-Nine

Before Perry, my apartment had been a typical bachelor pad. In other words, it was a mess. Once Perry came into my life, I'd stayed on top of keeping it straight for when she came over. She'd been gone from my life for almost a week and my house had suffered as much as I had.

The new décor of the room was brown—as in cardboard—due to all the empty pizza boxes. I'd thrown myself into work, already approving five new games for the company to produce. Jude's mom, Annie, had come knocking a few times asking for help with Jude, but I turned her down, unable to face him in my condition. The guilt of letting her down made me call Dawn and introduce them. Being a former school teacher, Dawn was happy to spend time with Jude and even offered to help him with his homework when Annie told her he'd been struggling.

Focusing on video games kept my mind off Perry. Well, at least I told myself it did. In truth, nothing took my mind off her. At night I pictured her lying beside me in bed talking over the events of our day. The first morning I'd convinced myself of her presence so strongly I had fixed her a cup of coffee.

"I'm losing my freaking mind," I'd mumbled after dumping the coffee down the sink.

Marie had been blowing my phone up with texts and calls. I refused to answer vocally, but I texted back so she'd know I was alive. After the first full day of dodging her, I started a daily text tradition.

Me: I'm alive. I haven't heard from Perry. I've eaten today. I don't want to talk.

Marie: I love you. I miss your voice. Please let me know as soon as you're ready to talk.

Dawn dropped off chocolate chip cookies with pecans at my door one day with a note that read, *We love you, Manny. Please come by soon. We miss you.* Brady knew best what I was going through. He left me alone, sending an occasional text letting me know he was there.

Ludington had been my home, but I'd never hated it until recently. Without Perry, I struggled to get out of bed each day. Things I enjoyed before barely mattered anymore. Even my work, which I loved, became monotonous. I still had so many questions. None of what happened with Perry in Tennessee made sense. Even after going over it repeatedly in my head, I couldn't make it compute. At the end of the week, I awoke feeling encouraged. Unsure of what came over me, I made the decision to call Perry. I wanted... no, I deserved answers. After touching her name on my phone and hitting send, I listened as the operator told me the number I'd dialed was no longer in service. "Fuck." My head fell back against the couch, I closed my eyes, and I let out a ragged breath. I missed her more intensely than I ever imagined I could.

After six days, I stepped out of the house for the first time. I breathed in the fresh air, sent a quick text, and rode my bike over to see my friends.

***

Dawn greeted me when I arrived to see Brady. She immediately pulled me into a hug. "How are you?"

"Where's Brady?" I purposely avoided her question. "I told him I was coming by."

"He had to run an errand. I'm supposed to meet him at the lighthouse for lunch. Why don't you come with us? I packed plenty of food." She had a basket sitting next to the door. "He didn't expect you home for a little while I think. Please join us?"

The pleading in her eyes made me cave. I needed friends around me. "Sure. Come on, I'll drive." The air outside was a chilly forty degrees, having a picnic seemed crazy to me. When we arrived at the lighthouse, I spotted Brady already halfway down the walkway.

"Go on down there and get him. We may want to eat in the car. It's a bit chilly out."

I left Dawn and walked down the concrete walkway until

I reached him. "Hey, Brady. Did you decide to propose to Dawn here instead? Otherwise, why are you having a picnic in almost freezing temperatures?"

He turned toward me and grinned. The next words I heard were, "Are you with him?" The same words Perry first spoke to me. Slowly turning around, my chest ached as my eyes landed on Perry only a few feet away from me.

"So, he's not your boyfriend?" she asked with a smirk.

"What? Him?" I point to Brady. "No, we're just friends. I mean, he's not my type. I'm… going to shut up." We stood there staring at each other, reliving our first moments together.

"I was afraid you'd left already." I couldn't keep up the act for long.

"I did. I was on my way to Florida. I have an apartment waiting for me and movers picking up my things tomorrow." I thought she'd be moving to another town in Michigan, not across the country from me.

"So, you're really leaving?"

"I was. And then I thought about everything that everyone has said to me in the last few days. The things Dawn said, what Marie told me, and your words went through my mind too. I couldn't leave without seeing you." She fidgeted with the hem of her shirt, dropping her gaze from mine briefly. I wanted to reach out and take hold of her hands.

"So this is goodbye?" Part of me thought it would have been easier if she hadn't come to see me again for a formal goodbye.

"That was my plan. For the last week I've been staying in

a hotel in Indiana. I made it to Indianapolis before the panic set in. I called my parents to let them know I needed to stay there a few days, to unwind. I told myself I needed closure. I convinced myself if I came back in and said goodbye to you in person it would ease the guilt." Tears glistened in her eyes, her voice filled with emotion. "But standing here with you now, I can't say it." There was a small gap of space between us. I stepped forward to shorten the gap.

"How'd you know I'd be here?"

"I called Dawn, and she told me." I looked back to where Brady had been. I'd been so preoccupied with Perry I hadn't noticed he left, nor had I noticed the picnic basket they'd left behind. I bent down to retrieve a note attached.

"Talk over dinner. We love you both," I read. "Love Dawn and Brady." In the parking lot, I could see them driving away. "I hope you have your car. It's a bit cold out here."

"I drive a Jeep. It's not going to be much better in there." She reached down to lift the basket, but I took it from her hands. When my hand grazed hers, she peered up at me, our faces only inches apart. I leaned in wanting to kiss her but stopped myself.

"We'll turn on the heat." I grasped her hand and led her to the car. Once inside, she started the engine. I went through the basket. "They packed us sandwiches, cookies, and chips."

"I'm not hungry." Neither was I, for once in my life. I closed the basket and placed it in the back seat. "I'm sorry, Manny," she began. "I only wanted what's best for you."

"Have you figured out the same conclusion I have on that one?" I asked. Her eyebrows scrunched together in thought. "You're what's best for me."

I grew tired of holding back, I brushed my lips against hers gently at first. When she placed her hand behind my head pulling me closer, I dove deeper. She tugged at my shirt while moaning into my mouth. "I love you, Perry."

"I know."

Chapter Thirty

PERRY

One Year Later

I pushed open the door and ran inside waving a piece of paper around. "Cancer free!" I exclaimed. Manny lifted me and swung me around. When he let me down, I saw the tears in his eyes. "I hope those are happy tears."

"The happiest, chica."

For the past year, we'd agreed to take things one step at a time. I stayed in Michigan, rented my apartment again, and changed my treatments to the hospital in a nearby town. Manny went to every single appointment with me. He held my hair and wiped my face when I got sick after chemo treatments. On the days when I thought all hope was lost and tried to push him away, he fought me and stayed close.

Two months ago, he asked me to move in with him. I had three months left on my lease and told him we'd revisit it once the lease was up and my treatments ended. I'd decided in my own mind I'd move in with him. Brady and Dawn got married last month. After the ceremony, Manny started talking about marriage. When he brought it up, I asked, "Are you proposing?"

To which he responded, "What would be your answer if I was?"

"Yes." And suddenly we were engaged. We picked out a ring together. I almost gave back the ring when I saw him with Marie's little boy, Eric, and her daughter Constance when they came to visit. Not because I was jealous of their relationship, but because I knew I'd never give Manny a biological child of his own.

After Connie's message about Manny making a great father one day, I thought for sure my prognosis for fertility would be better. Instead, her message led me to taking the pregnancy test and going to the doctor just in time for me to have a greater chance of survival. Connie saved my life, even if the initial thought scared the hell out of me. Manny and I have talked about adopting one day too. Being a parent with my level of anxiety was a terrifying thought, but I knew Manny would be a perfect dad. For every fear I voiced to him, he had a solution to calm me.

No matter what I did to push him away, he fought to stay. I knew I'd never have someone love me the way he did. He gave me the great love I'd written about, but I never thought really existed.

"You never gave up on me."

"And I never will," he swore. After making him promise to leave me if I asked, and then holding him to his word, I knew how strong his promises were.

The End

Thank you

Thanks for reading *Finding Your Way*. I do hope you enjoyed Manny and Perry's story. I appreciate your help in spreading the word, including telling a friend. Before you go, it would mean so much to me if you would take a few minutes to write a review and share how you feel about my story so others may find my work. Reviews really do help readers find books. Please leave a review on your favorite book site.

Don't miss out on New Releases, Exclusive Giveaways, and much more!

FOLLOW ME ON TWITTER:

WWW.TWITTER.COM/AMYTHAMCCLUNG

FOLLOW ME ON PINTEREST:

WWW.PINTEREST.COM/AMYTHA22

FOLLOW ME ON GOODREADS

WWW.GOODREADS.COM/AUTHOR/SHOW/

6421342.AMY_K_MCCLUNG

FOLLOW ME ON INSTAGRAM:

WWW.INSTAGRAM.COM/AMYKMCCLUNG/

VISIT MY WEBSITE FOR MY CURRENT BOOKLIST:

WWW.AMYKMCCLUNG.BLOGSPOT.COM/

I'd love to hear from you directly, too. Please feel free to email me at amy.k.mcclung@att.net or check out my website https://amykmcclung.blogspot.com/ for updates.

Acknowledgments

First, to that handful of readers who have enjoyed every one of my books, I love you and you're the reason I keep writing! Thank you for loving these characters, my family, as much as I do and inviting them into your life!

To my editor, Peggy – you're amazing! You pushed me to reach deep down and write things which terrified me, experiences with my own anxiety – the thoughts that make me feel crazy every day. Your suggestions helped me to strengthen this story beyond what I could have imagined. I appreciate you more than you can ever know!

To Ashley C– your spirit and personality just bring a smile to my face and to everyone who meets you! I can't thank you enough for reaching out to me and offering to beta on this book. Your feedback filled in blanks I hadn't considered and added so much to this story. You're awesome!

This writing journey of mine has introduced me to so many people I can't name them all, but I love each and every one of you. For my Hot Tree family – Becky, Olivia,

Justine, ALL the amazing authors and editors – I couldn't do this without your support and encouragement. You guys are the best!

To my mom, who is the only person in my family to have read every single one of my books. Your support means the world to me!

And last, but in no way least, to my amazing husband, Daniel. Manny's patience and loving nature is modeled completely after you. You talk me down when I'm in a panic and you hold my hand when I need support. You encourage me to keep going no matter how often I want to give up. I love you and I couldn't imagine my life without you in it.

About the Publisher

Hot Tree Publishing opened its doors in 2015 with an aspiration to bring quality fiction to the world of readers. With the initial focus on romance and a wide spread of romance subgenres, Hot Tree Publishing have since opened their first imprint, Tangled Tree Publishing, specializing in crime, mystery, suspense, and thriller.

Firmly seated in the industry as a leading editing provider to independent authors and small publishing houses, Hot Tree Publishing is the sister company to Hot Tree Editing, founded in 2012. Having established in-house editing and promotions, plus having a well-respected market presence, Hot Tree Publishing endeavors to be a leader in bringing quality stories to the world of readers.

Interested in discovering more amazing reads brought to you by Hot Tree Publishing? Head over to the website for information:

WWW.HOTTREEPUBLISHING.COM

9 781925 853544